TONTO SHORT STORIES

TONTO SHORT STORIES

edited by **PAUL BROWN**
and **STUART WHEATMAN**

tonto press

www.tontopress.com

CONTENTS

THE GOOD LITTLE WIFE
by STEPHEN SHIEBER

EACH Sunday evening the nuns made them kneel and pray before the granite statue of St. Catherine of Siena, the convent's patron. She towered over the girls, in her flowing robes, throttled by her wimple and pierced by a crown of thorns – a wedding present from her heavenly bridegroom. During her life, Catherine's crown was invisible.

All of the pain and none of the glory.

She never complained, said the nuns.

She never had the chance, thinks Kate.

Silence is always expected of women.

Still, there isn't time for such thoughts today. Kate must stay focussed. Ensure nothing is overlooked.

The devil is in the detail, Katherine. The devil is in the detail.

Kate shakes her head, ridding herself of her husband's voice. She has his lists to hand. They're bad enough, without one of his little maxims dogging her.

Kate crosses each item off her shopping list, scoring out her husband's neat, controlled handwriting. Salmon. Star anise. Cinnamon sticks. Melon. Parma ham. Wine. Gin. All present, all correct, spilling out of the bags on the back seat of her car.

She crumples up the shopping list and drops it into the clean ashtray. Next is the dry cleaning. White shirt, suit, dress, napkins. Kate places the list on the passenger seat and accelerates off.

Inside she is all rebellion, a fiery anger that threatens to consume her, to plunge her into hellish visions of revenge. Gripping the steering wheel until her knuckles blanch, Kate parks carelessly and runs across the road clutching the dry cleaning ticket in her left hand.

The girl in the shop is indifferent to her presence, greets her with a practised half-smile. Kate sighs. She is doing her job. Fulfilling her education. A young lady is seen and not heard. A woman runs her home with an invisible touch. Nuns glide silently down corridors.

Spectres of womanhood.

Grabbing at her clean items, in their clear plastic bags, Kate's fingers meet the assistant's for a moment. The softest of touches. Kate shrinks back, draws herself in and shivers.

'Thank you.'

She cannot disguise the quiver in her voice. She slopes back to the car, crushed, shoulders rounded.

Time to return home.

She launches the dry cleaning list on the breeze. It soon becomes a distant speck as the Mercedes roars away.

From the rear-view, Kate surveys the heap of items on the back seat. Essential ingredients for a perfect dinner party. Flowers, food, drink and costumes. A disordered pile that would drive her husband mad. Sometimes, she wonders if it isn't him that attended convent school.

Back at home, Kate places the salmon steaks into a roasting tray, sousing them with white wine. She scatters star anise, chunks of fennel and cinnamon sticks over the top. Why he picked salmon, she doesn't know. It always needs excuses making for it.

But he knows best. The head of the household. Andrew Allsop, the honourable man. Devoted to wife and job and church.

Kate takes a slug from the open wine.

At school, she always felt an affinity for St. Rita, the patron of desperate cases. This nun had a vision of the crucified Christ, during which he removed a thorn from his crown and pierced her head with it. There it festered. Very soon, the wound stank so badly that her fellow nuns moved their cells away from hers.

What a thoughtful husband.

Friends from the early days of her marriage now avoid Kate. They all have children. Are busy with school runs and party runs, trips to bowling alleys, swimming pools and pizza restaurants. For a while, perhaps, these women reserved her a space at the school gates. Until it became clear that Kate would never catch them up. Now they cast frozen smiles from the safety of their people carriers. Or wave stiffly from their Range Rovers.

If they see her on the street, they walk by on the other side.

She doesn't complain or protest. It's not what good women do. Not women with fine houses, industrious husbands and plenty of spare cash. Such blessed women must accept drawbacks.

After all, into each life a little rain must fall.

Melon balls splat on the floor. Kate comes to her senses, angry at the mess she has made. Tonight must be perfect. The boss and his wife are coming. A promotion is in the offing.

And I deserve this, Katherine, I really do.

Yes Andrew, and a lot more besides.

Kate spends half the afternoon arranging sweet peas in crystal vases. Bronze Chrysanthemums in moss green coloured pots. Crimson rose heads float on water for her table's centrepiece.

She folds napkins like an Origami mistress, grateful that her education has not gone to waste. As she fashions Japanese Cranes from Irish linen, Kate feels a little thrill of excitement curling around her stomach. She resists its pull. Feelings are nothing, a long-dead nun whispers hoarsely. Love is proved by actions.

Kate builds the canapés lovingly, spooning mounds of dark eggs onto blini cushions and topping them with sour cream. She pipes chicken mousseline into dainty pastry shells, wondering which poor bitch had the monotonous job of creating them. Kate takes the sharpest knife from the block and shards carrots and cucumber. She arranges everything on a tray and steps back to admire her handiwork. Andrew has had her too cheap. She should have received a pay-rise years ago.

Satisfied, Kate wipes her hands on a tea towel (another thing Andrew hates her doing) and takes a peek in her handbag. Yes, the ticket is still there, in its little cardboard folder. She flips the folder open and checks each detail again, just to be sure.

She went to town for it, in dark glasses, scarf and hat. Almost wimpled. She paid with her own credit card, one Andrew knows nothing about. A little fraudulence provided her with it.

All the way home, she checked her bag every couple of minutes. As if the ticket could grow legs and give its Vuitton prison the slip.

She has no definite plan for Edinburgh. Perhaps she will go back to the convent. Kneel once more before the statue of St. Catherine of Siena, and beg forgiveness for the wasted years of her marriage, for her silent submission to all this.

'I, too, have suffered...'

Kate's voice jars in her ears, echoing in the huge, gleaming kitchen. If the walls could talk, there would be no need for this evening's feat of bravery. She feels dizzy simply contemplating her nerve.

Kate runs a bath. She lowers herself carefully into the scalding water. It bites and pinches her skin, turning her pink, like cooked salmon. She gasps and squirms until the dull pain matches the ache in her ribs.

Fixed to her dressing table mirror is Andrew's 'last minute' list. Mix Martinis. Fill ice bucket. Remove canapés from fridge. Smile. Be charming. Obedient.

As if she had any other option.

Six years of marriage won't be wiped away in a stroke.

Kate snatches this final list down and shreds it. She places the pieces in her bin and sets light to them. They glow briefly and then turn to ashes.

They dated three times before he kissed her. A quick peck on the cheek. He was the One, all love and respect. She accepted his proposal without hesitation.

The fairytale lasted until their wedding night. In the honeymoon suite, he stripped her and pinned her down with his knees.

She thought it was a game. A kink of his, until he pushed his fist into her mouth and bent back her wrist until it snapped. An accident he murmured, as he forced his way into her.

When he finally fell asleep, she wrapped her robe round her trembling body and wept silently into her hands.

The day's cocktail of champagne, beer and red wine was, apparently, too much for him. It would never, never happen again.

She wanted to believe him. Just as, years before, she wanted to believe that St. Catherine's crown of thorns was a blessing. So, Kate held onto this belief that her obedience would calm him.

Four miscarriages and a hysterectomy later, she has reached the end of her tether. Faith is a childish thing. Maturity requires it to be put away.

Drying her hair, Kate smiles at her reflection. After faith comes wisdom. Now she plays him at his own game. Guilt is a powerful motivator. So, instead of love, care and self-respect, Kate has a material life that most women would kill for.

She feels a vague ingratitude for throwing it away. But she is hungry for something more, something less likely to fail. The Mercedes' engine has a recurring fault. Constantly updating her wardrobe seems a terrible responsibility. Apart from a necessary nose job, she hasn't had a beauty treatment for years. It's impossible for her to sit the day out in a swimsuit.

Would you catch St. Catherine or St. Rita in a jacuzzi? Or a mud and seaweed wrap?

The door opens behind her and Kate starts up.

'Hello darling.' He grazes her cheek with his lips, casting an appraising eye over her body. Andrew has been careful since he first floated the idea of this dinner party. She has no bruises above the tops of her breasts.

'Show me the dress.'

'I'm not ready yet, Andrew. Later.'

His left foot taps against the bedroom floor.

'Show me the dress, Katherine.'

The air fizzes between them, ready to blow. Kate stamps down her rebellious urges, the desire to throw it all away now. To slap him in the face with her credit card and train ticket. She drops her robe, treating him to an eyeful of his handiwork. She lingers over pulling on her knickers and tights.

'No bra,' he asks coldly.

Kate smiles softly, 'Not in this dress.'

Andrew pulls the dress off its hanger and gathers it in a bunch over her head, waiting for her to raise her arms like a child. Kate resists the urge to wince as her ribs ring with pain. She smoothes herself down and steps into her heels.

'Jewellery?'

She hasn't prepared for this. Panic beads perspiration across her forehead.

'The pearls?'

Andrew cocks his head to one side, waiting.

Silence thickens around them, a silence in which Kate gropes for the correct alternative.

'If you want to wear the pearls, Katherine, you go ahead and wear the pearls. Why make a special effort for me?'

She wants to grab him, to sink her fingernails into his fleshy cheeks, until he squeals like a pig. Until blood flows down his face, for a change.

She should knee him in the balls. If she could find them.

'What about the emerald necklace, darling? I bought it to

complement your wedding ring.'

Kate searches her jewellery box. 'Yes, yes of course.' Why she didn't think of it before? The emerald was expensive. She could pawn it.

She extracts the necklace and lets Andrew fasten it for her. His breath tingles on her neck. Kate freezes, until he steps back.

'Hair up or hair down?'

'Hair up, of course, Katherine.' Andrew hands her a jewelled clip and the silver brush from the set he bought her last Christmas. Kate watches in the mirror as he undresses.

The kitchen knife would slide easily through his flabby white torso, crimson blood staining the greying ladder of hairs between his chest and navel. Sighing, Kate rises from the stool and excuses herself, muttering about checking the salmon.

'But what about my back? I need my back soaping.'

The air ignites. 'Andrew, darling,' she begins, not convinced she has the strength to go through with this. Her tongue may flop, limp and useless, before the words are out. 'Andrew. You can pull your own cock while you're in the bath.'

'What?' he roars at her, keeping his distance all the same.

'If you like, I can tell Mr and Mrs Lennon that dinner is ruined because I had to wank you off, like a good little wife.'

Thunderclouds cover his face. Kate crosses the room, witness to her own bold display. She kisses him on the cheek and takes hold of his right hand, cupping it against his tightening crotch.

'God gave you hands for a reason. Put this one to good use.'

Kate refrains from adding, 'For a change.'

Andrew watches open-mouthed as she leaves the room.

The guests arrive at eight o'clock precisely. Andrew is mixing Martinis, polishing the glasses, tipping olives into a bowl.

Kate checks herself in the hall mirror before she opens the door. She wonders if she should let the top of her dress slip a little, whether they will notice the tooth marks on her breasts. Perhaps if she takes the emerald off...

'Mr and Mrs Lennon. Lovely to see you.'

Kate steps back to let them in, feeling Andrew's arm encircling her waist. His weight and height offer her a moment's security, transport her back to happier days. A wave of love for the man he was, for the woman she was, surprises her. She struggles to retain her balance and falls back into him, crumpling his suit.

He lifts her like a feather, setting her down in the direction of the kitchen.

Oh yes, the canapés. The performance of her life. She never was much of an actress. In school productions, she was happy to blend into the chorus.

Sister Constance tried to encourage her forward. Now, there was a performer. That thousand-watt smile, morning, noon and night. The Mary Poppins of the convent. But, ever so occasionally, when Constance thought no one was looking, her smile devolved into a serial killer's grimace.

Kate lifts the tray and pushes open the kitchen door with her free hand. The sitting room is filled with the false laughter and polite conversation that is the currency of their marriage, their frequent entertaining. Making sure her own smile hasn't slipped, Kate offers the tray to Mr and Mrs Lennon. She is vaguely aware that the salmon is beginning to burn.

Mr Lennon wipes his dry, puckered mouth and turns his attention to Kate.

'So, my dear, how would you feel if Andrew was promoted? It would mean a lot more trips away, not all of which you'd be able to accompany him on.'

Kate mentally scans the good wife script to find her line but, before she can speak, Andrew jumps in.

'Katherine's utterly supportive of my career. Aren't you, darling?' He doesn't wait for an answer. 'She's a very good wife like that. And she certainly benefits...'

He gestures to the room around them. Kate blushes. Lennon coughs. Before her St. Catherine appears, frowning and crumpling a train ticket to Edinburgh in her right hand.

'Actually, Mr Lennon, Mrs Lennon, I wanted to talk to you about Andrew's promotion.'

'You do?' This is Mrs Lennon, looking like a startled bird. Kate flicks a glance at Andrew, whose face mirrors the old woman's.

It's now or never, thinks Kate. She rises, unzips and wriggles out of her black carapace. She submits herself to their scrutiny, feels positively pornographic as the old couple shuffle forward in their seats.

Kate lifts her arms to display the bites on her breasts, the way her lily-white skin is pocked and scarred. She feels Andrew's shadow fall on her, hears his voice as if underwater, smells the charring fish. Her burning skin is cooled by the frozen gasps of Mr and Mrs Lennon. Two pairs of eyes scan the garland of livid bruises across her torso. Satisfied, Kate turns around and rolls down her tights so they can fully appreciate the extent of the damage a lit cigarette end can do.

But the silence is awful. She begins to sing, to fill the yawning void in her living room.

'*I feel pretty, oh so pretty...*'

Above her song, Andrew roars. St. Catherine's granite forehead starts to bleed. Mrs Lennon rushes forward, grabbing up the discarded dress, using it to shield Kate's breasts. Kate shudders and moans. A thousand thorns pierce her repeatedly.

Strong arms encircle her and lift her up.

There will be a fire if someone doesn't turn off the oven in a minute.

Mrs Lennon rushes down the hall to the kitchen as the men carry Kate upstairs. The world lurches and rotates and she wants to vomit. They hold her too tightly. Resistance is useless.

Later, they stand over her, cooing softly. She tries to open her eyes, but her lids are too heavy.

'Poor darling,' says Andrew, stroking her damp hair, 'you've been under such pressure lately.'

He turns to look at Mr and Mrs Lennon. 'I had no idea… I can only apologise…'

Lennon waves the apology away. 'Maybe it's time you concentrated on her, Andrew. The poor girl needs looking after…'

As they shuffle out of the door, Kate hears them reassure her husband that all will be well. That there are therapies, cures, for problems such as hers.

She waits for Andrew to return, reading her script again, more than familiar with the next scene.

The back of his hand strikes her face with renewed force. Kate bites her lip to stop herself from screaming. Tomorrow they will take a trip into town and get a refund on that train ticket.

BOOKSHELVES
by JOLENE HUI

I was in the middle of straightening my books when I smelled
the burning chicken flesh. Kundera by Vonnegut by ancient
Greek textbooks by anthologies by Jude Deveraux...

'Hey, do you smell that?' Tom shouted from the next room.

'Uh, yeah...' Shakespeare by Dickens by Faulkner by *Com-
munist Manifesto* by Fannie Flagg. I could hear Tom running
across the condo to the kitchen.

'Sonofabitch, shit!' screeched Tom. Raymond Carver by
Margaret Atwood by Joyce Carol Oates...

'Goddammit!' Tom screamed so loud the pastor next door
probably had a heart attack while planning his sermon. Danielle
Steele by Helen Fielding... The burning smell was filling my
nose and smoke drifted across my eyelashes.

'What is that disgusting smell?' I turned my neck towards
the kitchen and saw Tom floundering about in the hallway with
oven mitts on his hands.

'What do you think is going on?' Tom's face was red and he
had sweat coming down his forehead. 'I asked you to watch the
fucking chicken while I was working on a new riff in the other

room. What the hell?' The sweat started to pour off his crinkled forehead.

'Hey, I'm sorry. I was busy. I forgot.'

'You forgot? You're closer than I am to the kitchen and you couldn't even get off your ass to turn the goddamned oven off?'

I turned back around to my new bookshelves and tuned out Tom as the smell drifted into the study. Where should I put the Latin textbooks?

'Are you even listening to me?' Tom groaned, threw the chicken and broiler pan into the sink and threw the oven mitts to the floor. 'I'm leaving,' said Tom. 'I'll be back later.'

I closed my eyes to imagine the size and shape of my new office at the community college where I had just scored a position in administrative work. My dream was to be a professor someday at a university where I could be like Michael Douglas in *Wonder Boys*. Instead, I had spent the past two years substitute teaching scrawny second-graders and sitting in coffee shops. I longed to be immersed in books and writing. Reality reminded me every day that at this point in my life, I really couldn't be too picky.

'I'm back.' The door slammed behind Tom's loud footsteps.

'Take your shoes off, you slob,' I yelled from the study.

I heard two thuds against the door.

'You're going to pay for that if you break any holes in it, you know,' I shouted from my study where I was now dusting the shelves of my newly arranged bookshelves with a Pledge grab-it that smelled like a Dreamsicle.

'Shut your trap,' yelled Tom as he marched into the kitchen and turned on the faucet.

I ignored his comment as I stood up and took in the view of my glorious bookshelves. Fifteen shelves of my most prized possessions – from literature to romance to mysteries to children's novels. I squealed with delight even with the clanging of dishes in the other room.

'Hey, you gonna get in here and help me,' screeched Tom in

an irritated voice.

'Uh, yeah, give me a minute,' I replied, carefully trying not to lose my temper with him.

Danielle Steele's *Granny Dan*, could not be by George Eliot's *Middlemarch*. I grunted and got back down on my knees. Suddenly I smelled the pleasant odor of steamed rice.

'What are you making in there?' I yelled into the kitchen.

'What do you think I'm making, smart one?' yelled Tom.

'Whatever.' I set down my flavorful dusting rag and switched *Granny Dan* with Donna Tartt's *The Secret History*.

I could hear the clock ticking above my head as I made the switch and stood up again. They looked fabulous. I walked a couple of laps around the room and stretched my arms above my head. I was just feeling relaxed when I heard the phone ring.

'Hello,' answered Tom.

I stopped walking and tilted my head toward the doorway to hear what he was saying.

'Tonight? Well, OK. I have practice tomorrow morning at eight. Other than that... er... no. Sure I can meet you tonight. If I can't I'll call you, OK?' Tom quickly hung up the phone.

I sat back down on the floor and then stretched out on my back and stared at the bumpy ceiling. I closed my eyes.

The phone rang again.

'Hello,' Tom answered. 'Hey, how's it going, man?'

My eyes popped open. Tom talked on the phone more than any man on Earth. Hell, Tom could be gay for all I knew. We hadn't had sex in weeks. I attributed this to the fact that he was having writer's block every time he picked up a guitar to compose, but there was still a lingering feeling of a lacking physical attraction.

'Sure. Well, I'm hanging out with John tonight. Do you want to come? Oh, OK.' Pause. 'Cool, then, well, call me sometime tomorrow.'

I broke my silence. 'Who was that?'

'None of your business,' Tom grunted.

'Why are you so mean anyway?' I whined and stood up, dusting my jeans off and looking around the room as I thought of what else to say to Tom.

'I'm not mean to you. I just wish you would leave me alone once in a while,' Tom said from the other room as he opened and shut cupboards.

'Where are you going tonight?' I asked.

'For a drink, why?'

'Can I come?'

'Why?'

'Because I was under the impression that I was your girl-friend and that we lived together,' I explained. 'Although, I could be wrong.'

'If you want to say something, why don't you say it to my face?' Tom's volume shot up.

'I'm not trying to say anything. I'm just wondering where you're going and why we don't go out anymore.'

'Get off it, OK?'

'Sorry. I'll just go back to what I was doing. It was more fun than talking to you anyway, you psycho.'

'You're calling me the psycho? You're the one who's been in there all day rearranging your books.'

'So I'm trying to be organized, what's your point?'

There was silence in the other room.

I rolled on to my side and looked at the bare wall in front of me. Another bookshelf would do, I thought and then rolled onto my back and stared at the ceiling again. The smell of steamed rice floated up my nose but I would not give in to Tom's bad mood. I started thinking about my new office. Which books would I set on my desk? Would a Judith McNaught novel be too cheap? Would it convey a bad message to the students? Maybe I should put a nice Norton Anthology on my desk accompanied by the AP guide... in case they wanted me to teach intro journalism classes or something. Yeah, that would be cool. Wait, who was I kidding? I would probably just be making copies for grumpy old professors with beer bellies and a permanent cigar stench on their old sports coats. I closed my eyes and smiled, thinking about having my own office. Having my own space. A novel idea, my own space.

'Do you want to eat or what?' Tom yelled.

I grunted loudly.

He said, 'I went to the store just to get rice to make fried rice because you screwed up the chicken so get in here!'

'No. I'm not hungry,' I lied.

'You're lying. I know you're hungry. You've only had yogurt today.'

'You're keeping track of what I eat now?' I yelled. I closed my eyes and thought about the movie *Henry and June*. Why couldn't I ever get into Henry Miller's writing? It was so incredibly boring. But the movie was great. Uma Thurman as the leggy June. Smoking cigarettes and...

'Hey, get your ass in here and eat!' Tom shouted again. 'I'm done eating and I'm cleaning up so it's your last chance.'

'Hey, don't throw it out, I'm busy in here,' I blatantly lied. 'I'll eat after I'm done.' He answered with the sound of a garbage disposal. I pulled my chest up to meet my knees and yawned. Surveying my bookshelves I realized that I had misplaced Fannie Flagg. I gently replaced her next to Jane Green. Hmmm. Jane Green was sitting right by Wendy Holden. I grabbed the dusting cloth and started at the top and worked my way down. My breathing slowed as I reached the bottom. The room was getting eerily dim as the sun set outside my window. The magenta streamed through the curtains and hit the shining bound books. A strand of hair fell down across my eyes. I sat mesmerized as the magenta turned slowly to black.

I heard the front door slam and I jumped up. Tom must have left to meet his friend. I took a last look at my books and stepped outside the room. I could still smell the lingering odor of fried rice drifting through the apartment. As I exited the room, I took one last look at my project. Everything seemed to be in order. Margaret Atwood was placed by Bram Stoker. The clock was pounding behind me. My heart matched the pace but began ticking furiously as I stumbled into the kitchen and groped for a light. My breathing became more rapid – I felt the switch and flipped it on as hard as I could. I slowed down my breathing and my heartbeat began to soften. I scanned the kitchen, approving of Tom's clean up skills. As my eyes shifted from one corner to the other, they were captured by a single blue plate sitting directly left of the stove. It was a plate of rice, artistically placed into a beautiful mound and carefully wrapped with plastic. I stepped up to the counter to notice a note fastened to the wrap:

I experimented a little bit. I thought it was good. I cooked in some bean sprouts and lettuce to give it some nutritional value. the little shrimp are there because you burned the chicken. Enjoy and I'll see you later.

Love, Tom

Even hours after he made it, it still smelled good. My stomach grumbled as I set the note to the side and stuck the plate in the microwave. As the low hum of the microwave filled the kitchen, I began to remember my childhood – going home after school and plopping down on my bed to read another *Babysitter's Club* book. I remembered my Dad waiting outside of the bookstore while I perused the *Nancy Drew* section. I remembered thoroughly enjoying Jude Deveraux's sex scenes at age eleven... I jumped when the microwave beeped. I sat in silence while I ate my rice, enjoying the hard work that Tom had put into my dinner. I thought about going to work on my books again, but then I realized that I was really tired and wanted to take a bath and go to bed. The lukewarm water cleaned my plate in a flash. I was soaking in bubbles within five minutes. And, damnit, I had forgotten my book. I could feel the bubbles forming a sort of grease layer on my skin, but it felt kind of nice and soft; soft and pleasing to run my fingers across my arms, they glided across my forearms and thighs so smoothly. I sighed and drifted off to sleep, dreaming about money, writing, and men.

As I crawled into bed, I stared up at the ceiling and heard the clock ticking in the next room. I pulled the covers up to my chin and gazed at the white curtains. My feet started to get cold so I leapt up to grab a pair of wool socks.

As an afterthought I ran into the kitchen and collected the note from Tom. I read it again, slowly, and smiled. I crept into the dark study with the constant beat and spotted my favorite book of all, *The Giver*, by Lois Lowry. I sat down, crosslegged, and carefully removed the book. Setting the book softly in my lap, I folded the note in half. I stuck it underneath the 'about the author' flap inside the book jacket. Closing it, I rubbed the cover, brought it softly to my lips, and put it back where it belonged. I strolled back into my bedroom, ignoring the clock, and tucked myself under my mounds of covers. Instead of looking at the ceiling, I turned onto my side and closed my eyes. I vaguely remembered Tom getting into bed, his warmth radiating my sock-covered feet.

DILEMMA
by SAM JACKSON

RONNIE took delivery of the inflatable woman with scarcely murmured thanks and quickly closed the door. The ginger-haired man with the contemptibly loud tie gave a cheery 'Cheerio,' to the mottled pane before him and, thankfully, disappeared.

Ronnie gazed at the effigy in his arms with a mixture of re-vulsion and extreme irritation. The things people donated to a church table-top sale these days, quite frankly, it beggared belief.

'This,' so the donor had said, 'is Penelope. Fully inflated but never used. Maybe they can get a fiver for her?' Really!

Bearing Penelope before him as though she were emitting the most putrid of odours he turned into the living room. Leaning her up against a wall, he sighed. What would Stella make of all this, though he knew? Stella cleaned for him once a week and Ronnie was all too aware of the utter contempt in which she held him. How would she feel about him when she clapped her disapproving eyes on Penelope; not to mention Helga and Dionne and Svetlana? He gazed morosely at each inflatable woman in her turn. It had been quite a busy morning; men mainly, although Svetlana had simply been abandoned on his doorstep.

He looked at his watch; almost ten o'clock. Stella would be here in half an hour. Stella with her nicotine yellowed hands and always a black cardigan to mourn the ousting of Margaret Thatcher as Prime Minister. Stella with her hard face, probing fingers and, when she really desired to know something, the propensity to shake Ronnie until all his internal organs were scrambled. Would she do that if she *wasn't* my mother, he wondered sometimes. Probably.

What should he do? He sat down and leaned back into the unforgiving sofa. He closed his eyes and wished for soft music in the background and a cherry brandy in his hand. All his adult life he'd been told that as a man he should drink whisky but the only time he'd ever had a glass was the night he'd been designated 'first foot' at his Aunty Peggy's New Year's Eve celebrations a few years ago. He'd actually been promised a cherry brandy as an assortment of podgy and bony fingers had prodded him out into the cold but by the time anyone cared to recollect he was still out there it was two o'clock in the morning and the cherry brandy had disappeared long since. So they'd pushed a whisky into his frozen hands with the comment that he was lucky to get it because Mr Butcher had barged in the back way to demand they turn the noise down at some time shortly after one so Ronnie's claim to being 'first foot' was forfeit.

The women had then made Ronnie watch as they got down to the serious business of partying. It had been a shocking and revolting scene and one that provided a backdrop to many of his later nightmares: over-ample bosoms lurching perilously over the edge of balcony bra cups several sizes too small and flabby unfettered buttocks jiggling either side of outsize thongs, veiled only by the thinnest of material. There had been no other men present that night barring the hapless Mr Butcher, who was found late the following morning, unclad, and with his head between the breasts of a grotesquely naked Aunty Peggy; bruised, scratched and partially asphyxiated but, miraculously, pulled out alive. Previous recipients of Aunty Peggy's sexual favours had, in the main, tended not to have been quite so lucky and Ronnie had had to pretend to stumble across their rigid corpse in the woods the following day whilst out walking a dog he didn't possess.

Still sitting uncomfortably on the sofa he contemplated opening his eyes. This was far from an attractive proposition and Ronnie made several unsuccessful attempts to sell it to himself. Perhaps a compromise would do the trick then, just one eye to start with? Would that be possible did he think, and which should it be, left or right? This necessitated further deliberation with the judge's decision being far from final.

The dull, remorseless sound of a vacuum cleaner in full sadistic suction hummed loudly through the wall from next door, tormenting him. Ronnie pushed one ear up against the side of the sofa and grabbing the lumpy cushion from behind his back, he pressed it firmly against the other. How on earth could a man think with her making that horrible din? She ought to be dragged out into the street, publicly battered to death with her own ironing board and left strung out on her whirligig washing line to swing in the wind as an example to other women. Men needed to be left alone and in peace.

The clock on the mantelpiece chimed the quarter hour. This was it. Ronnie had to act. He opened his eyes, threw the cushion to one side and shot up from the sofa. After the dizziness subsided he knew he had to put a plan into action. The inflatables stared at him from all sides of the room, hard and unblinking. 'Bitches,' he thought. This was a truly grotesque situation and he cursed those responsible.

'Is this what the word *bric-a-brac* means to you?' he said loudly to an imaginary man by the battered bookcase.

Obviously he had to hide these things, but where? Stella didn't consider any part of her son's dreary abode to be off-limits, particularly his sock drawer, which was regularly interrogated for pornography, even though the sauciest thing he'd ever possessed was a wrongly addressed Damart catalogue and he'd only gone as far as making a small hole in the cellophane wrapper. No, today's was a problem of truly epic proportions.

He could let them down, of course, enjoy watching them crumple in on themselves; stand on their heads to force the air out more quickly. His eyes flickered. What fun!

But then this still presented a problem. He would have to locate the stopper in each woman and prise it out. The very thought repulsed him and he considered whether he ought to hyperventilate or dive straight into a full-blown panic attack at the very thought. He opted to hyperventilate. It was still fairly dramatic but would be quicker as he was now very short of time. And anyway, Ronnie's panic attacks whether full-blown or semi had never met with anything other than Stella's whole-hearted disapprobation and an unnecessarily vicious slap across the face.

Ronnie hurried into the kitchen, hyperventilating just as he'd seen people do in so many dramas on the television. He pulled open a drawer and rummaged frantically for a brown paper bag, his breathing increasingly laboured. After several hideously long seconds he spotted what he was looking for – but it was white. Why on earth had he held onto a white paper bag? In every film and TV series he'd ever watched everybody always hyperventilated into a brown paper bag. This was ridiculous. He must have a brown paper bag in there somewhere. He did. He knew he did, kept especially for these episodes of his. After a further two minutes of intensive searching and laboured breathing realisation suddenly struck him. Stella had removed his bag from the drawer; thrown it into the bin more than likely the spiteful cow. The penny dropped with a resounding clang and the shock returned his breathing to normal.

He looked down at the plastic carrier bags, wire ties and old bread bags now littering the kitchen floor. 'If I was an idiot female,' he thought, the bitter taste of venom flooding his mouth, 'that would be considered a work of art and *worth millions, dahling*. But I'm a man so it's just a mess on the floor that I'll have to tidy up or there'll be no... no... no what?'

Usually a man would say, 'No sex.' But this penalty didn't apply to Ronnie, it never had. He wouldn't want sex anyway. He had his television, his growing collection of DVDs, free with the *Mail on Sunday*, which was good. Now all he needed was the offer of a free DVD player and someone to connect it up for him. In this latter respect it was unfortunate for Ronnie that he had no friends. Male neighbours had long since stopped coming round; in fact some of them had made a point of moving away from the neighbourhood entirely. He therefore filled his days watching television and indulging in his passion for letter-writing – always letters of complaint. He wrote very frequently to his MP. He also wrote to the local newspaper editor, the Headmaster of the comprehensive school whose pupils walked noisily passed his door during *Countdown*, and Mr Heggarty the proprietor of the local newsagents who refused point blank to stock Ronnie's favourite magazines. The thought of taking out annual subscriptions for these publications and giving his details to complete strangers had been unthinkable, so Ronnie did without and hated Mr Heggarty.

His only other form of employment was as a volunteer for the church and it was in this capacity that he had offered his home as temporary storage space for donations to the forthcoming table top sale. It had been a proud moment for Ronnie when the Reverend Salter had announced his name for this particular honour and a quite shocking moment for the rest of the tiny congregation. Ronnie had beamed broadly though the vicar somehow missed him as his eyes roamed among his flock.

Nothing of much interest was anticipated. However, Ronnie had prayed with all his might for the safe deliverance of a dusty Faberge egg, an undiscovered old master, or a rare first edition, all of which would be 'lost in transit', as Ronnie would say later, subtly alluding to Mr Heggarty's green Transit. The newsagent also did voluntary work for the church and, much to Ronnie's annoyance, garnered far more praise from the Reverend Salter for his efforts than he himself ever did.

Ronnie turned away from the debris on the floor, determined to leave it there for once and to hell with the consequences. He needed a drink. He glanced at the kettle but gave it short shrift. Today was an exceptional one. It had started off exceptional and would continue all the way through in much the same manner. Ronnie began to feel excited. He smiled, clapped his hands together and strode the three paces required to place him at the exact opposite end of the kitchen. He glanced round just to check and listened for the slightest sound of a key being inserted into the lock. Nothing. Quick as a flash he had the bottle of cherry brandy in his hands. Out came the stopper and down his throat the liquid went. There was no other alternative. He'd explored every avenue and this was the only way out of his predicament. He lowered the bottle and dabbed at the corners of his mouth with one shirt cuff and wiped his eyes on the back of the other. This was no time to observe the social niceties. There was a deed to be done and Ronnie was the man of the moment. He gulped down more of the brandy, even dribbling some purposefully down his chin and onto his shirt as tangible evidence of the urgency of the situation and to reinforce that today was totally different from any other day in his life.

The clock in the living room sullenly chimed the half hour. This was it. There was no time to lose. Grabbing the largest knife from his knife-block, for surely no other implement would do, he leapt into the living room, grabbed the first woman and plunged the knife into her head. God it felt good. His heart raced, his face flushed, he yanked the knife back out and let her crumple to the floor. Why hadn't he done this sooner? It was so simple, so easy. Delightedly, Ronnie grabbed the next woman and plunged the knife in, slicing down from the nape of her neck to her buttocks in one quick and easy action. Dropping her to the floor he trampled her in his rush to get to the next one. Straight through the heart this time, pow, and she was gone. He'd slash the face of the next one he decided and did so. That would show her. That felt good. Exhilarated, he moved on to the next one. Her vagina. She had it coming, the bitch. Leaning her over the back of the sofa he thrust the knife straight up between her legs and revelled in the ecstasy he felt. This was wonderful, marvellous, fantastic, clearly the best day ever of Ronnie's life.

The vacuum cleaner suddenly switched off next door and there was silence. He'd made it just in time.

Still breathing hard, Ronnie looked at the knife in his hand and smiled. Then he looked down at his blood-soaked shirt and his smile became a laugh; on and on it went, louder and louder, tears soon streaming down his cheeks. He dropped to his knees still clutching the knife and giggling. Then as carefully as he could he plucked a shred of black cardigan wool from the blood-stained blade and lifted it triumphantly aloft.

NINE LIES
by ROBIN MARSDEN

(i) BEGINNINGS

I KNEW that I would be disappointed even before she started, because of her sad smile while she was tucking me in. I closed my eyes and waited to feel her nose rubbing against mine, but as it did, I could still picture the expression on her face, and something about it worried me. After five rubs to the left and five to the right, she asked:

'Now would anybody like to hear a story?'

I answered that I would more eagerly than usual, sensing that our routine was at risk of being broken.

'Ah – Katherine would like to hear a story,' she continued, 'And is there any particular story that Katherine would like to hear?'

'The one about the crocodile!' I said, patting the book by her side. She paused, closed her eyes and inhaled sharply.

'Then we'll read that one,' she said in a quiet voice. 'But... since Grandmother is staying with us, maybe we should ask her to read it to you. Now what do you think about that?' I noticed that she sounded far from convinced, and I knotted my face into my best scowl. I was shocked to see that this turned her stern.

'Now you will behave yourself for your grandmother, and you'll listen to her just like you listen to me,' she almost shouted. 'Alright?'

I nodded, doing my best to look confused and abandoned. She stood up and strode from the room.

When she came back she was arm-in-arm with a woman who I only recognized when she was lowered into the armchair by my bedside. She looked smaller and more fragile than last time I had seen her, which hadn't been that long before. She seemed to be thinking about something else, and she was panicked by Mum's explanation of what she would be reading: my favourite part of *Peter Pan*. This was a story that she knew, it was explained: the part at the Mysterious River where they meet the crocodile and learn why it makes that eerie ticking noise.

Grandmother cleared her throat with a rumble that gradually overtook her, and the book gradually slid from her lap. Mum picked it up and handed it to her, showed me another sad smile, and then left the room with one hand covering her mouth.

While Grandmother sat and composed herself, I began to examine her. I noticed that her hair did not look like hair at all, but rather some finely-spun silver thread that glowed with its own light. I was fascinated by the ripples of skin that travelled easily over her skull, and I watched them move back and forth as she squinted at the book, moving it closer and further away from her face. When she had it in focus, she looked across at me and, happy that she had my full attention, started with Chapter Five.

'Feeling that Peter was on his way back, the Neverland had again woke into life,' she began. As she continued, I strained to hear the words, but in contrast to Mum's secretive whisper, her voice was a monotonous mumble. I knew that she was not going to use a baritone for Captain Hook, or a wild-eyed whisper for the sound of the clock as it went, 'Tick! Tick! Tick! Tick!'

'...licking its lips for the rest of me,' she continued, and I realised that I had not been listening to her for some time.

Suddenly, I realised what I had been listening to: another sad story, taking place elsewhere in the house.

I had heard Mum's muted footsteps as they moved across the landing carpet and made their way down the stairs. But when they had reached the first step, I had heard them stop. That was where she was now, perched on the edge of that step, listening to my Grandmother's voice as she read.

Just two nights ago, I had been sitting on that step too. While I listened, my father explained something to Mum in the voice that he always used when he was worried that one of us was going to cry. They had been talking about a letter that had arrived from the hospital for Enid, and only now did I realise that Enid was my Grandmother's name. This would explain the low moan she let out when he had finished, and why they were silent for such a long time while I crept back up the stairs. Now, my mother would be on the same step, tucked up with her arms around her knees, listening to her Mum read a bedtime story.

'Some day the clock will run down, and then he'll get you,' Grandmother continued in her whispered tremolo. 'Hook wetted his dry lips. "Ay," he said, "that's the fear that haunts me."'

I readied myself for the moment the story finished. If she got to the end, I wanted to look like I'd just heard it for the very first time.

(ii) QUESTIONS

Joe's mother ushered us into the silent sitting room, where the rest of his family lay in wait. She motioned for us to stand side by side, opposite the glowing fire and Joe's furious father. He stared fixedly at us, his bald head the unforgiving colour of mahogany. In the armchair next to him sat his daughter, crumpled and wronged. Next to her, reclaimed by the family aura, sat Joe.

'When I speak about this disgusting business to your parents,' Joe's father pronounced, 'and to the school, tell me: how do you advise me to begin?' He started hard at Davies. 'Am I to maintain that Jonathan Blight and my Joe were mere accomplices? And that this Davies character was entirely responsible for the... violation?'

Hearing this word, Sarah let out a theatrical whimper and squirmed in her seat. In her new position she looked even younger, her spotless shoes pointing towards each other to underline her innocence. If only she had been standing up it would have been more obvious that she was three years older than Joe, Davies and me.

'Well?' Joe's father demanded with a sudden, parade-ground roar.

Davies' chin began to quiver, and his eyes and mouth tightened with tears. He looked round at me, then gave two fait nods. He began to cry.

'Sorry, Mr Stevens Sir, but it wasn't like that,' I interrupted in a surprisingly shrill voice. Everyone turned to look at me, and I took a deep breath. 'I touched her too,' I continued. 'I mean, we both touched her Sir, me and Davies. When she'd taken off her skirt...'

And her blouse,' added Joe, with a solemn nod.

'...It all seemed to be a big game.'

Joe's father was a trigger's width from exploding, and his gaze bulged with energy. Something about that taut expression reminded me of Joe, the way he had looked when we were all following his sister in a silent line. I looked now at his father's face, and I began to wonder if his energy felt the same as ours, under his skin. The same as when Sarah had held out her hand for our pocket money, and asked us, 'Now which one of you boys is going to be a man...?' Or the same as when she had pulled the square of yellow silk aside to reveal a pale, goose-pimpled breast.

Joe's father closed his eyes and began to speak in a low voice, struggling to control himself.

'By rights, I should have you *expelled* from that school, and your fathers then would beat you black and blue...' His eyes remained closed as he considered this possibility. He was breathing quickly. 'But I cannot have the reputation of my daughter soiled by a pair of young criminals like you. I shall call in on your parents, and inform them you have both had a violent incident... with my Joe. Then we shall see how long it is before you see your pocket money again.'

With an expression of challenge and then triumph, he looked around the tiny living room. While Davies sobbed with relief and Sarah lifted a hand to cover her smile, I asked myself what stopped me from talking. Why did I let Joe's mother's hand rest on my back and guide me out the house, instead of turning round and telling him that we had all touched and kissed Sarah? That it was only my disgusted reaction that had made her swear her revenge? As Davies and I waved weakly at Joe and walked on in silence down the street, why could I not turn back and tell her father how she'd paid for those spotless shoes?

(iii) PARTY TIME

At first, I was astonished when she asked me for help. Decorating the hall for the leavers' dance was a task that many girls coveted, and I had no idea why Susie had chosen me. As I watched her group sneak out of the dining hall to smoke behind the gym, it occurred to me that she usually went around with older girls, all of whom had left the previous year, and maybe that was why she was short of helpers. People had started to take more of an interest in me recently, but then they always did immediately before the exams when they wanted to copy my notes. Susie was popular all year round, thanks to her cigarette-card good-looks and her knack for saying things that made the teachers blush. We seemed to have so little in common that I didn't really know why she'd chosen me, but I was certainly glad of the distraction on that long final afternoon.

While everybody else sat outside, shoeless and lazy in the afternoon sun, we worked our way around the stuffy hall with a crate full of decorations. After a spell of excited chatter, we had all become silently absorbed in cutting lengths of ribbon or blowing up and bunching balloons. I had hoped that I could be of some use to the slower girls, showing them how to tie the balloons so that no air escaped and they would all be the same size, or how to twist the ribbon so that more of it caught the light and it shimmered as it moved. However, Susie didn't seem to be interested in my suggestions. She just kept shouting 'Ribbon!' or 'Balloons!' and immediately someone gave her what she wanted. When we had been in there for nearly two hours, I decided to make a final proposal.

'When we've finished the side walls, don't you think that we could brighten up that dull old thing?' I said, pointing to the clock that was mounted behind the stage. I said this largely for Susie's benefit, as she herself had persuaded the headmaster this year to allow a more cheerful colour scheme, replacing the maroon and gold of our school crest with flame red and a sizzling yellow. There was more riding on her success than there had been in previous years, and maybe this was why she simply glanced at the clock and said:

'Mmm… maybe if there's time at the end. Right now, there are more important things.' I nodded and returned to bunching my balloons, trying my best to find ones that were roughly the same size. But I could only do this for short spells without the same thought coming to mind: when we had all looked up, the time on the clock had been nearly a quarter to three. And this meant that if Johnnie Blight was going to ask me, he only had half an hour left.

I'd been careful not to tell anybody that I wanted to be his partner, as I knew that my fragile hope might easily be broken. All of the girls in our year agreed that Johnnie was very handsome, but most of them were put off by his rather intense shyness, and I'd been the only one patient enough to coax him into conversation. When I'd asked him earlier in the week if he had any plans for the dance, he had looked particularly nervous, constantly smoothing down the hairs on his forearms and looking everywhere but into my eyes. I had taken this as a promising sign, and every time the door to the hall swung open, I turned to look if it was him. Each time, the figure that squeaked across the polished floor was not the one I wanted to see, and each time the clock above the stage showed that more of the afternoon had gone. When we hung the last loop of ribbon between two bunches of balloons, Susie turned to talk to us from the top of the step ladder, and my hopes began to change colour.

'Well now,' she said, 'this is starting to look like a place where a girl might have some fun!' One by one, we all stepped back to take in the full effect, and our eyes widened as we were struck by how much the dull, dusty gym had changed. Thanks to the colours that Susie had chosen, it looked to me to be a different room, one that should be filled by people much more glamorous than me.

'So of course,' she continued, 'you've all got someone coming to call when the clock strikes eight tomorrow?' When nobody answered her, she turned to me and said 'What about the mysterious Katherine, for example?' For the first time, it occurred to me that I might be considered mysterious by these loud, lipsticked girls. I felt myself colour up, but her friends looked at me with encouragement, obviously eager for my reply. I looked up at the clock, which said ten past three; five minutes until the end of the day. I was starting to consider telling them about Johnnie, when Susie's eyes followed mine, and I was surprised to hear her say:

'Oh Katherine, I'm so sorry, you were absolutely right!' As we all looked up, she strode towards the stage with the step-ladder under one arm and a bunch of balloons under the other. Once she was up there, she unfolded the ladder and began to climb. When she had reached the top, she turned to her audience and said, 'I now declare exam time officially over. From now on, it's… party time!'

With this, she wrestled the clock from the wall and replaced it with the bunch of balloons. All the other girls seemed thrilled by this, and I reluctantly joined them in giving her a small round of applause. Looking at the clock, I had realised why she'd had me helping her all afternoon. I knew then that there was no point in waiting to see if Johnnie would come. When we had finished clearing up, I declined the girls' offer to come with them. Instead, I left all my things in my locker and snuck out of school on my own. I was sure that everyone would be impressed by our decorations, even though I wouldn't be there to see them on the night. I didn't want to watch Susie come in with Johnnie Blight on her arm.

Rather than waiting for the school bus and re-joining everyone else, I decided to walk into town in the early evening sun. Before they all came shrieking out of school, the streets were warm and silent, and I started watching my shadow as I followed it home through the town. As it moved over the softening concrete, the shape became distorted, and it gradually got longer as the sun moved down through the sky. By the time I got home, it was such a strange shape that it no longer seemed like my own.

(iv) THE PARTY'S OVER

When Susie first announced that she wanted to have a party, I worried that I knew why. For the last three weeks, I'd been desperately revising for my end of term exams, and I'd hardly seen her. By the way that she stumbled around when she came home in the early hours of the morning, stopping on the stairs to suppress a giggling fit before she flopped into bed next to me, I judged that she wasn't missing me too much. Although she still gave me a warm kiss when my alarm clock went off and I left her in bed, I was convinced that she was more interested in other people's company. When she barged into the library on a Thursday afternoon and reeled off a list of who she'd invited, my fears seemed to be confirmed.

'…and Graham of course, and Tim Wiseman… and that friend of his. Danny!' As always, she immediately brightened up the room, and I noticed the librarian looking her up and down as I led her out into daylight.

'And Ian!' she continued loudly, 'and that tall chap. Robby is it? Or Rob. Anyway…' Each name reached me on a wave of spirit fumes, and when she lost her balance and suddenly found herself sitting on the lawn, she let out a squeal of glee. I thought that maybe now would be as good a time as any to say what I'd been planning about her drinking. But then she looked up at me and flung her arms open, and I felt as lucky as I had when she'd asked me to the high school dance.

'Oh and Johnnie!' she shrieked when I knelt down to hold her, 'I forgot the best thing of all! It's fancy dress!'

Over the next two days, I tried my best to persuade her that this was a bad idea. She told to me that the theme would be 'The End of an Era,' to fit in with the end of our first year at university and the close of the decade that had given us the Vietnam war and the Kennedy assassination. I wanted to ask her to come inside and let me help her with her costume, but I knew that she wouldn't reveal what she was making until it was perfect, and so I left her in the garden, alone.

Three hours into the party, and I still felt ridiculous in the outfit she'd made me. I fought a path to the bathroom several times, to stare with revulsion at the hair that seemed to surge out of my underpants, on which she had stuck a fig leaf made from green card. Susie, of course, looked terrific as Eve, and each time that I came back into the garden with a fresh beer, a different crowd of men were standing in a circle around her. Every so often, I heard a 'Ta-daaa!' and looked round to see her twirling in front of some Roman soldiers, silent movie stars, or Aborigines clutching their didgeridoos. I couldn't hear them above the noise, but by the way that they were pointing at her and nodding to each other, I could tell that they were all impressed. She had judged the costume perfectly, so that the carefully-cut leaves only just obscured her white bra and knickers. It was impossible to look at her without imagining the warm skin beneath those leaves, and as she bounced around the garden welcoming newcomers, I was sure that this was what most of them were doing. I was probably the only one who noticed how much more thinner and more fragile she was now than she had been at the beginning of the year, her sharp bones visible underneath the pale skin.

Suddenly, I felt a pain in my side, and it took a second to register that someone was poking me.

'Who'd have thought you could make that out of one of your ribs, eh?' he drawled loudly, gesturing towards Susie. He was standing uncomfortably close to me, wearing a plain black suit, white shirt and black tie. Aside from a small birthmark near his right temple, he was enviably handsome. He cast his charming smile around the room, lingered for a while on Susie who was encouraging the people around her to form a can-can line, and then turned back to me.

'You know, she's just about perfect mate,' he confided. 'If I were you, I'd be the happiest man in the world. How's about another drink?' With his empty glass, he motioned for me to lead in to the kitchen, and I turned sideways to make my way through the shouting guests.

When we got to the table, sticky already with spilled drinks, he found two used plastic cups and poured us both a vodka. I usually stopped after one or two so that I could look after Susie, but for some reason that I didn't know yet, I'd been on edge all evening, and so I squashed my plastic cup against his and drank.

'I've never been round this neck of the woods,' he confided loudly, 'but I bumped into Suze in the Carpenter's and she said I should come along.' He began to fill our glasses with another shot, and I pictured her, working her way around the gloom of the afternoon pub, tempting complete strangers to our tiny house. I raised my cup again, gulped the vodka down, and leaned back against the wall. I was sure that she was happy, whatever she was doing, and it struck me that perhaps this was the most important thing. Whatever she wanted, if it wasn't me, then who was I to stand in her way? I was just beginning to feel sick at this thought, when the guy in the suit slapped his hand down on my shoulder and beamed at me earnestly, trying to project his smile onto my face.

'Listen, mate,' he said gravely. 'Great party.' With this, he poured me a third shot of vodka and raised his cup to me. 'Funny really,' he added, pausing to down his drink, 'you'd have thought that shooters would be the last thing I'd want to see!' With that, he put down his cup and turned to go back outside. Only then did I see the ketchup that was clogging the back of his hair and realise that he was supposed to be Kennedy. I don't remember much about the party after that.

When I woke up to go to the bathroom during the night, the house was strangely quiet: filled with the smell of stale drinks and the chattering silence that a party leaves behind. It was me that found her on the bathroom floor, with the empty pill jar and a bottle of the same vodka by her side. She had folded up her costume carefully and laid it on the corner of the bath, and it struck me how peaceful she looked, like a child who had just got ready for bed. Seconds later I was calling an ambulance, and while they were pumping her stomach in the hospital, I called her parents to tell them what was happening. With surprising calm, her father noted down my road directions.

At the end of that week, two days after he had driven her back to their family home, it was him who called to tell me that she wouldn't be coming back next term. His manner was warm, but something in his tone implied that the game was up, as if we'd all known that she couldn't make it through university and now it was time to stop pretending. He told me that she'd done this type of thing before while she was at school, and reassured me that no one would ever have known then either. He advised me to wait for her to make contact, but the summer and then the second year passed without a single letter or call.

A week after the party, I packed all of my clothes into a suitcase and moved out of our room. There were only a few things that I didn't put in – some large scented candles, some rainbow-coloured rolling papers, and our fancy dress costumes, which I left in the bottom drawer of the wardrobe. At the start of the following term, I smiled to think of the new arrival sliding it open to find them there, like relics from a time long gone.

(v) HOLDING HANDS

When Johnnie proposed inviting Graham, I could hardly say no. I mean, they've known each other for such a long time, and Johnnie has always thought of him as a good friend. I felt a small stab of poison in my stomach when he actually mentioned the name, but I wrote it down as quick as I could and we continued making the list. I'd already made so many compromises to get the whole thing off the ground, and I tried to see this as just one more.

The first had been the hairdresser, who'd asked me at the last minute if I'd mind having that new girl, the one with peroxide hair. She has a face like she's been sucking lemons, and she's so pale you wonder if she ever eats, but they've been good to me there over the years and I couldn't really say no. Then there was the food. Josie went to all the trouble of inviting us round for dinner before she asked if her friend could do it, the one who's apparently thinking of starting up in catering. Whatever happened, I just didn't want a scene like there was at Josie's engagement party, when the buffet was so bad that her Mum drove to the Post Office in town and came back with a carrier bag full of mints to hand round to everyone. I'm sure lots of people were still thinking about that buffet when they talked to Josie at our party. You remember these things, of course you do, even though you pretend not to.

As it happened, we can count our blessings. The food was fine, and the staff from the Marriott Hotel were fantastic. There was only one moment when it could all have gone wrong, but luckily nobody noticed, because Dad was in full flow with his speech.

He'd told a few stories about all the words I invented when I was little, and how he once caught me kicking the wall so that my toes would go flat and I'd be better at ballet. When the ripples of laughter had died down, he started with the serious bit. For all of that part, he had his body turned towards Johnnie and me, but I noticed that his eyes were looking straight down at the floor. When he finished by saying, 'Katherine is the thing that I am most proud of in my life,' you could tell that everyone was moved. I think that even he seemed a little surprised, and for a while he just stood there with a resigned smile, looking as if something terrible had just happened but we all had to put on a brave face.

Standing there while everybody else looked at him, I remember having the impression that this whole thing had nothing to do with me. I felt like I hadn't really understood what was happening until it was too late. Now my dress was itching, my satin shoes were biting into my feet and I was holding Johnnie's hand and smiling, there seemed to be no way out. I glanced around the room in search of some encouragement, and that's when Graham's face leaped out at me. And as soon as I saw him smiling, I remembered the last time that we were together.

We had been standing out on the damp lawn, holding onto each other for what seemed like hours. While I closed my eyes and listened to our kissing sounds, I felt that some kind of drunken warmth was keeping me safe from harm. Then Graham moved my hand downwards and started pushing himself against me. I took a small step back to discourage him, but he followed me without opening his eyes, groaning to himself and staggering towards me. He looked so much like a zombie, and I'd had so much to drink that must have let out a little laugh. I can see now that that was my mistake.

'What? You...' he said, his eyes springing open, angry now. Then something happened that made me lose my balance and I was suddenly facing in the other direction. With one hand, he held both of mine behind my back, and with the other he yanked at my tights. It all happened so fast that somehow I couldn't speak, and when he started pushing into me, I tried to think about anything apart from how much it hurt. I just remember looking straight down at the grass and feeling him squeezing my hands, letting them go and then squeezing them harder with the same rhythmical insistence. Suddenly it was over, and I brushed myself down, my hands red by then and trembling. I watched Graham walk back towards the light of the hall, and before he had even got inside I started to make my own way back, wondering at how easy it would be to walk back inside and carry on with everything.

When the silence broke and the applause began, I took in a sharp breath and everything came into focus. I followed everyone's eyes and saw that they were still looking at Dad. I've never told him, of course, and I've never told Johnnie; I can't imagine how much it would hurt them if I did. While the clapping continued, I squeezed Johnnie's hand and looked Graham straight in the eye, returning his uncertain smile. From now on, I remember thinking, I will be Mrs Johnnie Blight, and all of this will be behind me.

(vi) LETTING GO

I'd been out of the office all afternoon, yawning my way through another meeting about the ring road, so I didn't find out until about half past four. When I got back to my desk, I found a note in the bubbly handwriting of Mr Barker's secretary.

Waters broke just before 13:00, took her straight to hospital. Don't worry, she's fine, we'll be waiting for you. Ken.

Immediately, my heart fired a flare of anger. I'd spent eight months listening to endless advice, from parents and yellowing library books, and yet here was one complication that I couldn't avoid. It wasn't that Josh would now be three weeks early, and I'd have to drive across town in rush-hour traffic to get to the hospital. It was the fact that Ken had been the one to tell me. I could imagine his voice when he dictated the message; the soft, self-assured tone that he used, the smiling air of inevitability. Although I'd never admitted it, these were the things I hated most about Katherine's father.

I patted my pocket for my car keys and walked unsteadily out of the office, nodding in response to the half-hearted moans of 'good luck mate.' I took the lino-covered stairs two at a time, and when I got into the brown Allegro, I was relieved to hear the engine fire. I managed to drive all the way to the exit barrier before I was stopped by the Friday evening traffic, which sat bumper-to-bumper, unmoving in the road.

The orange hands on the dashboard clock read ten to five. I wondered what Kate was doing at that moment, and I was shocked to picture her face wrenched by pain. I looked around, and the woman at the car in front of me seemed to give up, slumping back into her seat and lighting a cigarette. In the car behind, a man in a suit was drumming out a rhythm on his plastic steering wheel, bobbing his head from side to side. I wanted to scream at them all to let me through, to tell them that seven gridlocked miles away, something critical was happening. Of course, they'd just have thought that I was a lunatic, waving his hands and silently screaming behind the windows of his car. Maybe they'd have been right, I thought. After all, wasn't I worried that my son was about to be stolen by my father-in-law?

As the car in front crept forwards, I started to think about Ken. Although we'd always been friendly to each other, this had been communicated by firm handshakes, brusque nods and bursts of too-loud laughter. Even at the wedding, when he'd slapped me on the back and slurred that he admired me, I thought I knew exactly what he meant. He wasn't happy that his precious girl had ended up with someone from the council traffic department. What he admired was the fact that I, like him, could make the effort for Katherine's sake. Standing there arm in arm, watching her as she danced to the disco music, we both knew that we had the same feelings butterflying round our bodies.

By now, I was maybe a mile from the hospital, in traffic that was crawling slowly. Kate must have been in labour for nearly five hours. As I drew level with the turn-off, I swore that at the next meeting about the ring road, I would give it my most vocal support, instead of thinking about my wife and worrying about my son. I had spent many hours spent in plastic chairs, thinking what books I could read to him or where we would teach him to ride a bike. Now I was convinced that it had all been a waste of time. How could I have been so stupid as to think that I could control this? I'd imagined a future that was smooth and perfect, where everything happened naturally. But here was the present, noisy and messy.

When I finally got to the hospital, reception called a nurse who took me straight to the room. With every squeaking step I took, a moment that had led to this flashed into my mind, from the first time that our hands touched when she was teaching me to shade in art class, to the time when her barbecue was torrentially rained off and, drinking wine in the attic as the roof pitter-pattered, I asked her to marry me.

The nurse gestured towards a pair of swing doors and gave me an encouraging smile. Before I went in, I peered through the small round window at the new world on the other side. Kate's head was propped up on pillows and her eyes were half-closed. She had half a smile on her face, and she looked like she was drunk past the point of caring. Standing by her side was her father, whose face had never looked more like hers. I followed his eyes down to the bundle in his arms, from which a tiny hand shot up and conjured a smile onto his face. I tasted tears at the corners of my mouth and raised my hand to open the door.

They both looked up when they heard me come in, and an exhausted expression of relief appeared on Kate's face. Ken, in contrast, looked alarmed, and he took a step backwards as I walked towards him, raising the baby up until it was nearly tucked under his chin. I stopped. From where I was standing, I could see that my son was perfect and healthy, and I understood why Ken would never want to let him go.

(vii) THE MISSING INGREDIENT

For me, the last two hours had been an oasis of calm, which ended abruptly before I even opened our front door.

'There you bloody are,' said Kate, shooting out to the car and grabbing all the carriers left in the boot. It was then that I remembered what I had forgotten, but I judged that I'd best keep it to myself. I took a deep breath, and followed her into the kitchen, which was alive with steaming pots and pans.

'And what about St Peter's? Don't tell me you still haven't rung them?' As she asked, she began to rifle the bags for lemons that she would never find.

'Err…' I began. She stopped moving completely.

'I'm sure that there are still places left for the open evening,' I said, noticing that the school's glossy brochure lay open on the dining room table. By its side was a very familiar-looking letter. I was sure that neither of these had found their way there by chance.

'Jonathan,' she said, closing her eyes. She looked like she was reading from a memorized script. 'If we're going to give Josh the best possible chance, then we decided that it has to be St Peter's. If you'd just try for a promotion we'd easily be able to pay the fees. And you know that Dad would be happy to help us, if only you'd let him. And after this…' She gestured towards the letter and then gave up, letting her forehead fall into her cupped hand.

The letter opened like so many other's we'd received from Josh's current school: *Although there has been a small improvement in your son's behaviour since our last communication…* I skim-read what remained and smiled at this latest illustration of Josh's comic initiative.

'I'm so glad you think it's funny,' said Kate. I picked up the brochure and, mustering a stern expression, strode decisively towards the sitting room. Behind me, she continued her search.

From the other side of the living-room door came the hoots and boinks of cartoons. Before opening it, I paused to look at the St Peter's brochure, the cover of which showed a wide-eyed young boy standing in front of a gate. Looming over him was a salivating old man, who was handing him a golden key. I sighed, folded the brochure roughly in half and thrust it into my back pocket.

I opened the door just in time to see a small, mean, blue character get hit in the face with a frying pan. With his tongue lolling out of his mouth and two crosses for eyes, he lost his balance and began his crashing progress down a never-ending staircase.

Josh heard my laugh, exclaimed 'Daddy!' and thrust both arms into the air. From the kitchen, I heard Kate's voice calling for my explanation. Just like I did every day, I wondered if I should leave her: just like I did every day, I wondered why she hadn't left me. I didn't know how it had come to this: lying so that I wouldn't have to send Josh to this horrific school, or not buying lemons so that her mussels would be ruined. I walked towards Josh, when behind me, the door opened and Kate cut me off.

'Daddy,' she said dryly, 'will you take Josh for a walk to get some lemons?' She disappeared again, and I felt Josh thunder into the back of my leg.

As I put on his shoes, Kate looked over me, with a stern expression on her adult face. Josh didn't look happy either – he could tell that there was something missing here. I led him out the door, swearing that I would do my best to make sure that this never happened to him.

(viii) ANSWERS

The first time that it happened, she screamed. It was the shrill bleep that shocked her, rather than the disembodied voice. Stranded by her housework – an assault course of shifted furniture to be cleaned underneath and behind – she listened to see what the plastic box would do next. She'd seen him setting it up, but since he hadn't found time to sit her down and patiently explain what it did, she was reduced to standing there rubber-gloved while it clicked into life.

'Congratulations,' it said in Johnnie's voice, 'you've reached the house of John and Katie Blight. I'm very sorry that we can't take your call at the moment. Please leave a message, and we'll get back to you as soon as we can.'

Hearing this for the first time, she felt a flush of pride. It was terribly professional to have one of these things, and the message that her husband had left just sounded so sincere. He really was sorry he couldn't take your call, she thought; he really did want to hear whatever the other person had to say. Clearly, they didn't share her feelings. After a pause, she heard them clear their throat and then clatter their receiver down.

While she waited for her racing heart to slow down, she wondered who it was. It couldn't have been Johnnie, who was at a conference in Leeds, and it couldn't have been Josh, because he'd have jumped at the opportunity to leave a message. Standing up with a click of her knees, she wrote the call off as a wrong number, and got back to her housework.

She'd spent most of Saturday morning in the living room,

lifting up and cleaning various objects they'd been given over the years. As she handled each one, she'd consider its contribution to the hidden story of her family. The slightly naff statuette of a ballerina had been a wedding gift from her father, its offensiveness mirroring his own feelings when his little girl had dared to grow up and get married. For nearly seventeen years, she hadn't been able to hide it behind something bigger and more tasteful, and so now it stood on top of the TV next to Josh's lop-sided pot. The pot, a more recent addition, told its own story; whereas Josh had inherited his father's flair for mathematics and organisation, her patient, artistic touch seemed to have passed him by. Standing there, doubled over as if it had been winded, the pot now served to embarrass their son whenever he brought somebody home, particularly when that person had been a shy, artistic girlfriend.

She put the pot down on the TV, and was about to start dusting the big screen when the phone began to ring. Immediately, she side-stepped round the back of the sofa and scooped up the receiver.

'Hello, Katherine Blight?' she said. This time there was a short pause before the line went dead. She wasn't sure how long it had lasted, but it had seemed somehow exact. She imagined somebody at the other end, nodding to themselves as they made a decision and then putting the receiver down. She started to wonder who this person was, then she was given another fright, by the slam and the shudder of the front door announcing the arrival of her son.

'Anyone tried to make contact, M?' he asked, popping his head around the door frame. He freed himself from his headphones and looked puzzled when she said:

'I'm not sure… someone called but then they put the phone down.' As she had feared he might, Josh picked it up, pressed a flourish of buttons and scribbled down a number on the pad.

'It was from London,' he said in his most businesslike voice. 'Looks like you were right, probably a wrong number.' He patted his stomach in a suggestion that she might make lunch soon, and then turned to leave the room, shouting gleefully over his shoulder. 'Unless of course you're having an affair!'

She was touched that he found this so inconceivable. She shouted in reply that lunch would be soon and got back to dusting the television.

This, with the ghastly satellite dish that stuck out from the front of the house like a zit, had been the latest addition to the room. Its purchase had marked a new stage in Johnnie's life that, to be honest, she was still getting used to. He'd bought them both to celebrate his promotion to Regional Traffic Director. He'd also upgraded to a new, faster car, which he drove up and down the country to presentations and conferences. Returning home exhausted late in the evening, he'd flop down on the sofa. Although she was curious about his new job, until now she'd always left him there to relax in front of the latest movie.

When she'd finished her cleaning, she put her clothes to wash and climbed into the steaming shower. Closing her eyes, she let out a long sigh as she bowed her head under the water. Then there was a sudden, desperate knocking on the bathroom door, and she spluttered and heard Josh's voice.

'Mum?'

'Mum!'

'The police are here, Mum! They said that they want to talk to you!'

She turned off the shower and dried herself carefully. She was sure that something terrible had happened and, catching her panic-stricken expression in the mirror, she took a deep breath and tried her best to look like a mother.

She came downstairs to find two black-clad policemen occupying her sofa. When she came in to the perfectly tidy room, they put down the cups of tea that Josh had made them and introduced themselves. The elder one said that Mr Blight's car had been involved in a serious accident. It had happened at a junction of the M25, heading towards West London. He said that often there wasn't any one person who was particularly to blame, but the severity of the impact did suggest that Mr Blight had been driving very fast. She put a hand to her mouth. The policeman was sorry to inform her that Mr Blight had been killed instantly, as had the driver of the oncoming van.

Later, when the policemen had left, she went straight to the telephone and tore the old sheets from the pad. She was sure that the number had nothing to do with this terrible accident. She was sure that the person clearing their throat had been a man and not a woman, and that Johnnie had just made a mistake when he'd said that his conference was in Leeds. As soon as she could, she would find the manual and work out how to erase the message. Then, as a family, they could begin to mourn Josh's father, who had been her faithful husband.

(Ix) ENDINGS

'I just can't see how it's all going to end,' said Simone, and the smile disappeared from Mrs Blight's face. Even though Simone had done the training course and gone over her notes with different-coloured highlighter pens, she was still convinced that some of the residents actually listened to her. The idea that they spent most of their time in some secret, interior world was hard for her to believe. She found it particularly difficult at ten o'clock, when she came round to Mrs Blight.

'Mmm... hmmm...' said the old woman, half-clearing her throat and shifting in her chair. Simone paused and looked up from the white cup into which she was counting tablets, tempted to see this as some kind of acknowledgement. She dismissed the thought with a quick shake of her head, remembering what they had all been told by Jocelyn, their training mentor.

'It's just like reading a story to kids: the important thing isn't what you say, it's how you say it. If you're loud and snappy, they know that you're angry. Soft and quiet, you're probably nice. It might look like they understand what you're saying, but most of the time they're just listening to your voice.'

As Simone had tried to put this into practice, she'd found herself looking forward to seeing particular residents. While several of them seemed to taunt her, smiling as they relieved themselves in the bed that she'd just changed, or dashing their dinner across the freshly vacuumed carpet, Mrs Blight actually seemed to enjoy her company. The old woman always looked relaxed in her brown velour armchair, and in the short time before she was wheeled out to the Day Room, she always let Simone have her say.

As the weeks went by, Simone had admitted to Mrs Blight that she found nursing difficult. She'd talked about her frequent trouble with boys, about one-night stands on sofas and in alleyways, wondering now and then what Mrs Blight had got up to in her day. Most recently, she'd taken Mrs Blight her latest pregnancy scare, the results of which seemed to have captured her attention.

'I mean, I can't decide if I'm gonna keep it or what,' said Simone, taking the blanket from over her legs, cos of course, that depends on whose it is.'

Rather than looking scandalised, Mrs Blight started making short, panicked glances around the room, looking for her hairbrush. Simone had already put it on her dressing table, along with her pearl earrings and a matching silver brooch. Simone handed her the hairbrush, and held up a mirror in front of her.

'It could be Dave,' she continued, 'cos I was still going round to his on Saturday nights back then if he texted me. But then I don't reckon it is, cos half the time he just got pissed and fell asleep. So it's probably Scott's. And that's alright, cos Scott's well fit. But then he's already got a kid with Charmaine.' Mrs Blight finished and put down her brush, which glowed with fine silver threads of her hair.

'I mean, I'd love to have a little one and everything,' Simone concluded, 'but there's other things I want to do with my life, you know?' With this, Simone lowered the mirror. She was struck by what she saw.

This week, for some reason, the formal blouse and the old jewellery made Mrs Blight seem much older. She sat straight with authority, filled with experience. At that moment, standing in front of the old woman in her blue carer's uniform that was slightly too big, Simone felt all the lightness of her nineteen years.

'I mean, I don't want to travel round the world or nothing,' she said, feeling suddenly foolish, pulling Mrs Blight up to pivot her round into the wheelchair. 'I just want to see if I can meet a lad who's actually... alright. Someone who knows how to treat you... and who's good looking, of course. You know, Mrs Blight, like your Josh.'

'Josh,' says Mrs Blight softly, her eyes widening, and she almost seems to smile. As she wheels Mrs Blight out of the room and down the corridor, Simone remembered what Jocelyn had said to them all: 'Even if the residents are looking right at you, they're usually thinking about something else. And it's probably for the best that you don't know what it is.' Simone walks past reception and on towards the lift, Simone trying to persuade herself that Mrs Blight is thinking about something else.

She leans the chair back to raise the front wheels into the lift, and as she does, Mrs Blight is thinking about her husband. She's thinking about his infidelity, and how she always knew that it would end their marriage, ever since they were teenagers and he asked someone else to the high school dance. As the lift goes up, she is thinking about Josh's last visit, when she briefly recognised that twinkle in his eye when he looked across the room at young Simone. Mrs Blight is sure that, by the time Simone reaches her age, the young girl's heart will have been broken a thousand times.

When the lift doors open, Mrs Blight's concentration begins to fade, and she scowls as she tried to hold onto a single, concluding thought. Nobody should be allowed to tell this girl what will happen, she thinks; nobody has the right to say that her dreams won't come true. As this thought forms and then slips from her grasp, her scowl slowly disappears, and Simone watches as it is replaced by a warm, contented smile.

Simone wheels the old woman out and into the Day Room, past Mr Patterson and Mr Rose, past Mrs Davies and Mr Stokes and on to her spot next to the polished table, which is sometimes folded out for dominoes. Simone reverses the wheelchair in and then bids her farewell, saying as she always does: 'See you later then Mrs Blight!'

This familiar sound occasions a broad smile on the old woman's face. For the first time, it occurs to Simone that what she's just said isn't true, that next time she sees Mrs Blight, the old woman probably won't know who she is. But it helps them both, Simone reckons, to end on a note of hope.

THE JELLYFISH
by FIONA CASE

THE sea in Cornwall can be very beautiful to look at, at its best on a clear summer's day, when it goes that bright deep blue – that blue which fills you with a sense of hopeful awe. A word, however, of warning: the water is, like enough, cold. Nay, *freezing*. And if it's not – if when you dip your questing toe, you don't wince and hop and clench your buttocks – don't bloody well go in. Because that's what the jellyfish like. And jellyfish have upgraded lately, what with all this climate change business, and, boy, you get some monsters out there. Twenty years ago, say, the jellyfish, when they came, were plentiful, but small, flexing through the water like translucent ladies' fists, their sting no more potent than the lively smart of nettle rash. They might even have been called pretty – or at least when you were in a boat, safe, out of the water. But now... well, even amply boated, you can't be *quite* sure as they parachute by.

You'll like them, though, when they wash up, as they do in numbers, rolling slowly and menacingly out of the waves, landing like upturned fruit bowls, turquoise in colour with tentacles, the shape of flippers, neatly frilled out round them.

Yes, you'll like them when you're on land in your unassailable element, and you can squat down and prod them with your finger, and be surprised how the top feels like hide, like leather, not the squoodge you expected. But don't turn them over, oh no – underneath is a gruesome mess of fleshly ruffs and tubing, which looks alive in an otherworldly, alien way. Underneath is pure horror.

***

Behind the sand dunes, sheltered by rose hip bushes, Marilyn, blonde and beautiful like the filmstar she was named after, was slowly removing her clothes, neatly folding each item, sobbing quietly as she did so, for her love had been abandoned, left naked and vulnerable, like a brain without its casing. As it had been before. The list of men with whom she'd had liaisons was *very* long, and quite diverse, but hopeless nonetheless. She was too beautiful, some said. And that was probably true. Always, briefly, she thought it would last forever; always she hoped. But it always did end – when the passion, however adamant, however eternal, sifted away like flour through a sieve.

'This es still a naturist beach, innet?' asked the old farmer of Susie.

Susie, all sarongly reticence, was crouching by a huge jellyfish, minding her own. And so engrossed was she by this beast, this thing, that she didn't immediately register what was being asked of her.

'Ay?' he hollered, thinking he'd missed something, cupping a beefy hand round an ear.

Susie jumped, and almost lost her balance. She steadied herself, then peered up at the weathered old face. 'Oh,' she said, 'I think I did see...' her eyes swept back down (quite of their own volition, she was powerless to stop them!) until they were level with... 'something. Oh.' She felt a shocking blush gush upwards from her neck. Not that she was an unworldly prude or anything. Indeed, she taught in a secondary school, so had seen it *all*. Rather it was the proximity of the grizzled and jowly genitalia, which dangled just before her nose, which disturbed and flushed her, and then primarily for aesthetic reasons.

But the old farmer wouldn't have understood that, after all nudity is only natural. And he thought perhaps he'd found a new friend. ''At a jellyfish, es et?' he asked.

'Yes,' said Susie.

'Ee's a size, in ee?'

Susie nodded.

'Never seen the likes afore.'

'No?'

'Never,' he confirmed weightily. After a few moments, he said: 'So, 'es es a naturist beach 'en.'

'I think it might be,' she said, not having thought about it at all.

'Don't see the point of no trunks.'

'No,' she said, very well seeing the point.

The old farmer was quiet then, though he continued to stand over Susie, his genitalia silently impinging upon her. And that presence, she found, diluted her curiosity; and the jellyfish was no longer able to command her full attention. After a minute or two she left it and wandered over to the water's edge, perhaps thinking to leave this strange character behind. But he followed.

Side by side they stood and stared ruminatively out at the horizon.

'Los' me fahther last yuur,' he said at length.

Susie turned to look at him. She met bright blue eyes, the colour vital and vivid like the sea just then, one of which bulged eagerly, suggesting the beginnings of benign insanity, as the other nestled quietly behind a drooping eyelid; she had the impression that if it suddenly began to rain the eyes would swap roles. Poor old thing, she thought, and said, with some feeling, 'I'm sorry.'

'Los' the fahrm, too – bloody inheri'ance taxes, innet. 'En me wife ran off.'

'How dreadful.'

'I miss makin' the 'ay.'

The good eye fixed Susie with glassy zeal, and she found herself avoiding it ever so slightly, staring instead at the wild scrubby eyebrow above it. What was she to say?

'I think that, that…' she started. But nothing apt was forthcoming. So she finished, 'I'd better go and put some suntan lotion on.' She turned slowly, sighed, then walked away.

He paused for a moment. But again he followed. He watched as she settled herself down on her towel; he twitched in memory of something quite rude as she squeezed lotion onto her legs; he voyeured as she smoothed and rubbed.

'Goes on a treat, dunnet?' he said finally. There was a touch of youthful breathiness in his voice.

Susie's brows knotted: she was *trying* to ignore him.

But how was he to know that?

'I'll put some on fur ee, if ee likes,' he said, his old eyes shining with teenage excitement.

Out of the corner of her eye, Susie thought she detected the slightest twitch. She flipped over onto her front and began rummaging in her bag.

'Well,' she said, and very loudly, her school-mistressy tones coming out, 'I think I'll read my book now, if you don't mind.'

'Oh…' Expectancy drained from his face. But he was used to *that*. 'Nice ta meet ee,' he said in a rather composed fashion.

The old farmer waddled off, his corpulent but stocky buttocks and legs bearing his mighty belly along, towards a small group, also bikini'd and trunk'd, a little further on. More friends, he thought, rubbing his hands together. He stopped, at encroaching proximity, put his hands on his hips and stuck his hirsute chest out grandly.

'Seen 'em jellyfish?' he asked after an almost indecent pause.

Marilyn removed her watch, sadly, laying it on the top of the pile: it caught the sun and flashed out so sailors might see it... oh, a *sailor*! But, no, it was too late for that. Just five minutes more... She picked one of the red rose hips and peeled the flesh away from the pouch of seeds within, wondering vaguely as she nibbled a piece and chewed if it were poisonous – not that it mattered particularly, and surely nothing that tasted so sweet could be deadly... She paused: it was always the sweet things in life which were deadly. She threw it, seeds scattering, away. Then waited impassively for violent death to take her: her mouth was primly closed, her long-lashed eyes fixed and glassy. But – some seconds passed, though it seemed much longer – she didn't appear to be dying. Perhaps it was slow-release poison. Perhaps, of course, it wasn't poisonous after all. Her eyes began roving again. It was as good a place as any. And she'd chosen it carefully, remembering it from a childhood holiday: it was as close to nature as she'd ever been, and she'd wanted to feel it for a second and last time. Though really she'd enjoyed the walk to this spot rather too much, pausing to finger crab apples, to admire the dainty white blossom of the blackberry bushes and the musty purple heather, which smelt so earthy, so *real*, and to gaze up at the rugged, dizzying cliffs. She wished for a moment that she'd brought her camera, but, well... how silly.

The strangest thing was it was so familiar. How did she remember it all? Not the names necessarily, but the images and smells? They roused something deep within her. She remembered something else, too, which passed through her like fresh clean air. Perhaps, after all, it wasn't such a good place. A flyover would have been better. There'd have been no remorse there. But what would one think in those few seconds of decent? Life must blaze by with blinding radiance, orgasmic brilliance. Wouldn't that make one want to live? What if she suddenly, a second in, say, changed her mind? How *dreadful*, she thought. Perhaps a shotgun would be best, but so terribly messy. A fly landed on her knee; she stared at it intently, noticing for the first time what a pretty thing it was, with purple honeycomb eyes, similar in hue to the heather, and elegant lightly veined wings and such delicate legs. The insect lapped at her skin; she tried to feel it, but found she couldn't.

The sea hissed lightly, rhythmically, calling; the tang of salt in the air beckoned. Yes, it was as good or bad a place as any. Three minutes and thirty seconds to go...

On the shoreline, three boys, ten or eleven years old, were running round the biggest of the washed up jellyfish, waving sticks and tapping their mouths rapidly as they released the Red Indian war cry of the old Westerns. When they tired of this, the preamble, they took turns to run in and poke their sticks into the 'hide' of the jellyfish. Rapidly their bravado grew. Until one punctured the surface. They drew back in shock, hands to mouths, delighted revulsion flashing in their eyes. Mesmerized, they watched the seawater gurgling and bubbling from the hole. They whispered. Then one of the boys approached, slowly carefully, and with his stick managed to roll the jellyfish over. Again they recoiled, this time with small squeals of pure horror. The thing looked alive in an otherworldly, alien way, as though it might jump at them and attach itself to their young torsos with a gooey life-bleeding suck.

But again the wonder, the macabre allure of pure yuckiness, drew them back in. First a gentle nudge. Soon thrashing and shrieking and laughing and egging, bits of tentacle flying...

The old farmer, who'd been watching the scene unfold with fascination, yelled encouragement: "At's it lads, giv'er some welly.'

But that stalled them. They squinted through floppy fringes, perplexity angling their brows.

'Uurgh,' gasped one, 'he's got no clothes on.'

'Someone's stolen his trunks!' whispered another.

'He's one of them, what do you call its...?'

'Dirty old man!'

'Paedophile!'

'Pervert!'

His hearing wasn't so good. But he understood. Insults were being tossed at him. There was no doubt: he recognized the exaggerated mouth movements, saw the way the form of the words and their intent diabolically snarled the fresh young faces.

'What!' he bellowed, 'I'll give *ee* some bloody welly.' He began jogging and stumbling over the sand towards them, waving his arms. They ran off, laughing, throwing taunts over shoulders.

Puffing and outrun, he soon gave up the chase, seemed even to forget all about it as he pottered over to the water's edge. There he stood, the mild surf lapping at his gnarled old toes, looking terribly flummoxed. A seagull screeched over, releasing a great ribbon of white shit as it went, which trailed down through the air and landed in an arc before his feet. He peered down at it: who'd have thought a bird could produce so much and why's it white anyway? The water licked away at it. They must be divine beings if even their shit is white. He looked mournfully out at the horizon, wondering, wondering; and took a couple of unconscious steps forward into the water.

Susie was the first to see Marilyn floundering and flailing over the dunes, making for the water. She watched her with a hard glint of apprehension in her eyes, but nonetheless with a certain feeling of inexplicable stomachy excitement, which tingled outwards, raising the hairs along her forearms and buzzing into her fingertips.

From a distance, three naughty boys watched.

'Here,' said one of them, 'she hasn't got any clothes on either.'

'Phwar,' commented another.

'Let's hide them,' cried the third.

'Hide what?'

'Her *clothes*, stupid.'

'Yeah!' they all cheered.

Marilyn was almost at the shore. In her side-vision, both to the left and right, she was vaguely aware of odd glassy glimmers, but she had no time to consider what they might be, as she plunged wildly into the frothing waves, not far from the old farmer.

'By God,' he said, as the desperate rush of hair and flesh sped past him, and the lithe legs began their mad high-step into the waves, 'she's a *booty.*'

Marilyn was soon waist deep, not much longer, she couldn't swim, but oh bloody hell, it'd help if she could, just to get herself *out*. She lunged and staggered and launched herself along, sobbing. Chest deep, almost there...

'*Aaahhhhahh.*'

The old farmer raised his hand, sailor-style, to his forehead. Susie sat up. The boys paused in their antics.

And then Marilyn was coming back, and at an even madder pace than she'd gone out, in fact, she was almost swimming, and screaming at the same time: 'Urghhh, stepped, *yuck*... giant... aaahhhaah... floating eye... eye... eye...' she bawled. She collapsed, mewling pathetically, onto the sand a few metres to the left of the old farmer's feet. When she opened her eyes, she realized with deepest horror that she was eye to eye with...

'*Aaahhhhahh.*'

The old farmer came forward and slowly lowered himself down, one knee at a time.

'There, there, my lovely, ee won't do ee no harm, not now.' He picked up one of the boys' discarded sticks and prodded the jellyfish. 'See, see, dead as a doughnut.'

'Duh-dough-doughnut?' Marilyn whimpered.

'Ay.'

Slowly the whimpering mutated into a gurgle, then a giggle, and then a deep wild laugh.

''Ere now, was the mattuh with ee?'

'Dead as a doughnut,' roared the girl, in braying hysteria.

'Ay,' said the farmer, 'ee is 'at.'

Marilyn stopped laughing and began shivering violently, and her teeth chattered.

'There, there, can't be as bad as all 'at. Ay? I'll look after ee.' He sat down beside her, took her hand and patted it gently.

'You're very nice,' Marilyn said.

They sat like that, quietly, two lost lonely souls, until the voice boomed out:

'What *do* you think you're doing? Come here *now*!'

Susie addressed the three boys, one of whom had a pair of ladies' panties pulled down over his head and was pretending to be a fighter pilot, running, his arms stretched out to the side, letting off a loud 'neeeeaauuum'; another who pranced campily in a bra which was back-to-front, twisted and upside down; and a third who had the rest of Marilyn's things clutched to his chest in an awkward embrace, and was making off along the dunes. At the sound of that voice, they recognized the tone all right, the boys were arrested in their activities, as though freeze-framed.

'Hum?'

They, heads hanging, shuffled, half-heartedly jostling one another, over the sand to her. They stopped just before her, and stood squirming beneath her fierce gaze.

'Sorry, miss,' puffed the gusset of a pair of ladies' undies, 'we didn't mean any harm.'

'Names?' Susie boomed.

'Alex,' said Alex, unpiloting himself.

'Danny,' said Danny, fighting the bra as he might a straight-jacket.

'Charlie,' said Charlie, struggling with dainties and shivering in the heat.

'I think an apology might be in order, don't you?' she announced. 'Then we'll see about what's to be done with you.' She swept her towel up with a flourish and marched off in Marilyn's direction. The boys trailed after her. 'And I hope you,' she trumpeted, with redoubtable authority, this time to the farmer, 'have been behaving yourself.'

'Not doin' no 'arm,' he replied sulkily.

'He's been very sweet,' said Marilyn.

'All well and good,' said Susie. 'Now let's get you covered up, shall we?' She began arranging her towel round Marilyn. 'And is there something you'd like to say boys?'

'We're…'

'Very…'

'Yes very…'

'Sorry?' suggested Susie.

The boys nodded glumly, holding out articles of clothing like peace offerings.

Marilyn blinked sadly at the boys, then began whimpering again. 'It hurts, it hurts,' she moaned, 'it bit me.' She pointed a accusatory finger at the nearby jellyfish, and rubbed her distressed calf.

'Oh no,' said Alex, 'it couldn't have *stung* you as it isn't poisonous.'

'You said they were very dangerous,' whined Charlie.

'Said it would eat us alive,' Danny chimed in.

Alex tutted and rolled his eyes theatrically. 'It. Was. A. Joke.' He turned to the adults: 'They're called Rhizostoma octopuses – though they are jellyfish – and they live on plankton. You see,' he said, prodding one of the flippers with his finger, they don't have tentacles as such: these are just mouth arms.'

The old farmer looked from the boys to Susie in confusion. Got to give it to 'er, he thought, she's got 'em little 'ooligans under control.

'But look, look,' groaned Marilyn, pointing to a rash on her leg.

'Oh dear,' said Alex, 'that must have been one of the little ones: they *do* sting. How does it feel?'

'Like I've got pins and needles, and it burns a bit too. And it hurts.'

'Don't worry about a thing,' announced Alex, all boyscoutly, 'I know exactly what to do.' And he was ordering Charlie – 'vinegar' – and Danny – 'flour… from the fish and chip stall, stupid' – and anyone (Susie as it turned out) – 'aftersun'. Feet puffed rapidly back and forth bringing ingredients. When all were reassembled, Alex began. He dusted the stricken area with flour, and scrapped it back off with the blade of a Swiss army knife – 'to remove any remaining stinging cells' – before dousing with vinegar ('Oooh,' gasped Marilyn, '*Ow*.') Then gentle fingers rubbed in the aftersun. 'There,' he said, quite the little GP, 'all better?'

'Much,' said Marilyn, with a bright smile, then added, 'My, you will be handsome when you grow up.'

Alex blushed.

'Well done!' exclaimed Susie. 'You've all quite redeemed yourselves. In fact, I think you deserve,' she paused for effect, 'an *ice cream*.'

'Thank you very much,' said Alex, 'But we've got to go now – because… because we're going to build a castle.'

'With a moat.'

'And a dungeon.'

And they were off.

'Oh,' exclaimed Susie, rather disappointed.

'Ice cream!' gushed Marilyn.

'It will be,' announced the old farmer, a tad histrionically, '*my* pleasure.'

'Do you think, first, that…' Susie paused. It was a delicate matter, she understood that. But there was nothing for it. 'Do you think,' she said gently, that you might avail yourself of some trunks?'

***

Cornish seaside life, on the east side at least, generally finishes early. Should you go for a walk at dusk – when the families who come, rolling forth from overheated automobiles to cover the sand with plastic belongings, have long since departed – you'll probably find yourself alone, no barbies, no beach parties; the sand will still be littered with detritus, with the pathos of human life abandoned; perhaps the odd faded crisp packet or carrier bag will puff listlessly past like manmade tumbleweed.

Find a pleasant spot, perhaps at the base of a dune. And watch how the tide gently and inexorably creeps forward – smoothing and soothing the puckered sand, licking the sharp edges of a broken bottle, brushing away cigarette butts. Further it comes, whispering enticements, its foamy fingers beckoning to the jellyfish, stretching for then reaching them, caressingly, tender and patient as a lover, by degrees mounting, luring and drawing these vast glittering jewels back into itself, reclaiming.

And tomorrow it'll be as if they never existed.

ELASTIC BELT
by PHIL JELL

WHEN I wrote 'one for every year of your life' what I meant to *say* was 'one for every year of your life *so far*'. I must get that straight right now; lay it down for your consideration. 'Be honest from the outset' they always tell you at the start of counselling sessions. I mention it because for me, going over these words has become something rather more than habitual. I wouldn't say I'm obsessed with it, but it really does matter a very great deal to me, and it's important to be clear about such things, wouldn't you agree?

Picture it: a birthday card, chosen with taste mind you, no cartoon cat or sickly ted, but an attractive, conservatively impressionistic Venice cityscape. Written very carefully – the message originally tested for form and content quality control on a sheet of fine writing paper before being copied into the card – and yet despite the fact that this is a 32nd birthday card, it is adorned with an endearingly immature sentimentality. For knowing how she loves and revels in my 'uxorious and quixotic devotion' (her words, not mine) I have played my part and come up with a fittingly naïve romantic gesture. 32 kisses, big and small. When I say 'kisses', I assume you realise I mean 'X's. Those impassioned ones that appear to have been scrawled in the midst of adulating ecstasy. And in parentheses below, to accentuate the smitten-simpleton effect even further, the language of naïve love we two privately re-appropriated for something more profound yet unsayable, I have written, in big, rounded, warm and simple letters, a simple rounded and warm message; 'one for every year of your life.'

Since last May I have thought about that last line continuously. I am trying now to think of a way to impress upon you just what I mean by that 'continuously'. I read once, in one of those spurious surveys in a women's magazine – and just to make the scenario even more absurdly banal I should add that yes, I was in fact in a dentists waiting room as I read it, though the appointment wasn't mine; I was picking up her sister's child from a minor brace adjustment session – where was I? Oh yes, I read, in this odious piece, that men think about sex three times a minute. Preposterous! Ludicrous! I disagree with it entirely. Clearly the article's writer was just trying to indicate how monumental the male libido is by anchoring it to impossible but fundamentally *graspable* statistics. But here's where it's useful as analogy; if I haven't thought about that sentence in the card three times a minute, I've certainly thought about it more than even the most frustrated adolescent boy has ever thought about sex.

And there I've given the key term. Sentence. Was it a sentence? Did it contain an imperative? Was I sentencing her? Am I responsible?

I was in marketing. Still am I suppose. They're keeping the position open, covering my Compassionate Leave with a temp, or something like that. Sending thoughtful emails and letters every so often. The obligatory cards. It's a funny thing how if it's a birthday, new baby, or even if you're leaving, you get one collective card; big and gross, semi-thoughtful signatures sprawled all over it. But something like this… Everyone wants to send one individually, dragging it all out, everyone revelling in the knowledge that *you* are suffering and not them, each wanting to somehow participate in it with you, to know what it feels like, but safely, from a voyeuristic distance.

Marketing. Not something I was ever passionate about, but something I had a knack for, and it paid well enough to support the lifestyle we enjoyed. Not a hard job. Evaluating strategies and trends, generating models for performance anticipated, scouting possible new sources of revenue, getting on the phone and knowing whom to phone. You can see, I am sure, the connection. In a word; prediction. I was very, very good at it. Yes. My predilection for prediction she used to call it. Your lecturer's love of alliteration, I used to retort. And we laughed.

I feel certain you understand what I am getting at now. When you put two and two together, what you get is always the same, after all.

I am good at prediction. I wrote a sentence that contained an incontrovertible truth. People say, 'Come *on*, how could you have *known*? It's an *absurd* link!' and I love to agree when they do, convincing myself they are right, if only for the short time they are actually with me. And yet, when you add together that capacity for prediction, and what was revealed as a very accurate instance of prediction, can there be more than one interpretation? Do two and two ever make three or five?

2.3 miles from our front door to her office at the university. I walk it about once a week now. Sometimes more. Not a long journey but she always drove, was always too late to walk, though she liked walking and kept on about how one day she would leave in enough time to do it.

So what do we have so far? A simple sentence, written as part of a foolish little game we played across the spaces of notes left for each other or special cards; melodramas acted out teasingly to acknowledge how unutterable our real love was. A journey of 2.3 miles. A date? But I told you; her birthday. Ah maybe I neglected… well it was the 18th. The 18th of May.

On May 18th, after she had left, that is after she had begun the journey of 2.3 miles in her little Volkswagen, I went to our bedroom and I changed my belt. The one I had put on earlier that morning was old and no longer fitted me very well, and a special birthday breakfast had expanded my stomach sufficiently to increase the discomfort I had not fully noticed before. But it suddenly reminded me of something, and the reason I say this is because I became so nostalgic, the memory so acute, that on that morning of May 18th I had tears in my eyes – real tears. A recollection suddenly wrenched from obsolete storage files, a memory delightfully alive and so close and present I could smell it.

A small boy. Me aged about five, maybe six. I owned a belt, and it was a belt that I liked very much indeed. It was elastic, striped dark red and blue, the lines following the belt's length around my tummy – I'd say stomach, but I was very small, and tummy is the definitive word at that age. Its clip was plastic; two halves of a chunky circle that clicked together to form a whole, and that whole held my trousers up.

One half of the clip was beige, one half dark brown, they joined in a straight line down the middle. When I first saw the yin and yang symbol later in life I felt that I intuitively understood it without needing to be told what it was; it was just a not-so-simple version of my belt.

What was most pleasing about this belt was the plastic click the two halves made as you brought them together. A big, solid, chunky sound. I liked that very much and I was always doing it up and undoing it; the plastic, being thick and strong, never broke. The little disc looked like a sweet, and always made me think of and crave sweets whenever I wore it, a round chocolate coin maybe, dark and white chocolate fused together in some wonderful chocolate shop, somewhere.

So I stood, nearly 30 years later, staring at the black leather strip in my hand, mentally superimposing upon it a smaller belt, elastic with a plastic semi-circle at each end that joined together to form a whole circle that reminded me of sweets, always made me want to buy sweets, though I never found any quite like it.

One day, once upon a time, long ago... (I remember a day, but not which day, so one day, once upon, long ago, must do) I had not used my belt for some time, feeling too grown up for it; I should think I was about seven years old by then. But on *this* day I was at home and decided to wear my belt again, remembering how much I liked it, and being aware that none of my friends were around to see me put on such a babyish thing.

I pulled it meticulously through each loop of my red corduroy trousers and pulled them up my thin smooth legs only to discover the tragedy. The ends would not clip together. I tugged and tugged, leaving thick red marks across my little-boy's-belly, but the ends would not meet. I struggled and wrenched, my thin little fingers going scarlet and shaking with effort until finally the clip clicked (with a rather sad, muffled and anticlimactic sound) and the elastic bit me so hard that I couldn't breathe, and I must have looked like an hourglass until I managed to claw it off again.

The first time I fully realised the irrevocability of growth; that I wasn't just happily and proudly getting bigger and all else remaining equal, but that I had to *lose* things as well, to leave them behind.

A belt superimposed on another belt. I chose the wrong words and the wrong belt that morning.

I have walked the distance to measure it exactly, and it was 1.2 miles to the very spot. They called me on the phone from 1.2 miles away, and caught me just as I was going out the door. If they hadn't got through, if they'd been a few seconds later, if I'd got the right belt, I would have been at work before I heard.

What's to tell? A truck. A driver hung over from the night before. The most obvious and painfully clichéd of scenarios; robbing me, in some absurd way, of an *original* sort of grief, belittling my feelings. A truck with a full skip on its platform. It wasn't her fault at all. She was a good driver, much better than me.

When I first looked at the birthday card again, a day or two later, I realised with growing horror my suppressed prescience, my imperative, my sentence. I realised that she had done no more than was implied; that her trajectory was plotted by my hand.

I'm not stupid. I know she didn't look at it and subsequently *decide* to die. But think about it this way. How many seconds to read the sentence I pronounced upon her span? How much faster out the door if it were not there at all? What if it lingered in her mind, caused her to slow, speed-up, whatever she did to cover 1.2 miles in exactly the wrong time? What if she realised my sentence just as five tons of steel ate into the little Volkswagen?

My friends say I 'dwell' on it unhealthily. In a few more months no doubt they will say I am obsessed, and probably call a lot less. Call on me a lot less, that is. They'll certainly call each other a lot more though, to discuss me. Can you blame them?

Can you blame me? 'So far'. Two words. A split-second. But a split-second later, a split-second that held her at a red light, pushed her through an amber one, waited for a car to pass, pulled out before one. Braked before a truck could... accelerated before a truck could...

Do you see? If I had not pronounced my final sentence, given my prediction before I was even at my desk and being paid to predict, she would be here. Right now. Today. Every day. See?

If you'll forgive a ludicrously melodramatic touch that I only employ because of a game I used to play with someone special, that induces an accompanying feeling I would very much like to invoke once again, I will add that in a few months there would have been another card (there might just be anyway, whether it will be read or not, though that all depends) with 33 kisses, 33 'X's dashed off as if scrawled in the midst of ... and below in parentheses, 'one for every year of your life, so far.'

Laugh at me all you want, if I seem absurd. I'm not trying to invent original sentiment here; I don't need to *market* this story to anyone. How can I help it if words seem only to reduce the potency of what has happened to me, to obscure my pain behind facades of cliché?

And that is the real point, isn't it? Every time I sit down to write this note, this note which keeps being torn up; the event postponed, I find myself incapable of saying what I must, of explaining myself, and I lose the will, or perhaps the courage.

And perhaps in a few moments I will go to the hall, unhook my looped belt from the banister at the bend in the staircase, and replace the tall chair in the kitchen, next to the breakfast bar, as I have on so many other occasions.

Perhaps I will even go back to work for a day or two, kidding myself that it might be bearable, but really knowing that what lies in store for me, what fills my only future, is to one day write the note that I am happy to leave behind.

Or perhaps I may even yet turn this note around; achieve the last words I need to find in order to undertake my little plan.

I don't want anyone to feel sorry for me. There's nothing to be sad about; the tragedy happened to me already. I'm only looking for a way to alleviate its effects. I'm lucky; I get to choose.

And yet so far, every choice that I think is made turns out to be elastic, stretches and changes, refuses to hold me in place, refuses to prevent my will from slipping down, and so I continue to search for the other sort of elastic belt, that will once again bite into me, and will not let go.

THE LUGER
by PAUL BROWN

PETER was beginning to doze when the knock came at the door. He opened his eyes and listened. He expected no visitors. He lived alone in a small flat in a suburb of Amsterdam and, since his retirement, he valued his solitude. Peter sat up in his high-backed chair and looked out of the window at the canal below. Rain pattered against the windowpane, and the tarmac on the streets was dark and glazed. Drops of rain met the surface of the canal like tiny pin pricks. There was no one in the street. No locals, no dog walkers, no tourists in brightly coloured raincoats. It was a grey day.

Another knock, louder this time. Peter grasped the arms of his chair and gradually raised himself to his feet. Of course he was not as fit as he had once been. Now the damp weather upset his knees and stiffened his ankles. Previously Peter would leave the flat every morning, to buy a newspaper or groceries, or to take a stroll by the canal. Now he would enjoy sitting and watching the world through his window.

Peter straightened himself out and slowly made his way to the door, past the old coffee table and battered sofa, and the tall display case containing his collection. The flat was old, the wallpaper peeling in places, but it was cosy and safe and warm. Peter stepped up to the door and put an eye to the peephole. A young man in a suit and raincoat was checking his watch on the stairwell.

'Who's there?' said Peter.

The young man coughed to clear his throat and said, 'I'm looking for Mr Voorjens.'

'Who are you?' said Peter.

'Oh, I'm sorry,' said the man. 'My name is Arnold Numan. I have something for Mr Voorjens. May I come in?'

Peter clipped the doorchain into its latch, unlocked the bolt, and pulled the door partway open. The hinges creaked and Arnold Numan smiled. His hair and shoulders were damp, as if he had been in the rain for only a short time.

'What do you have?' said Peter.

Arnold tapped the brown leather briefcase at his side and said, 'It's all in here, Mr Voorjens.'

Peter thought for a moment. The young man's shoes were spattered with rainwater, and he beamed widely through the door crack.

'Do you have any identification,' said Peter.

'No, Mr Voorjens,' said Arnold. 'I'm not from any official body. I'm from... Can I let you see?'

Peter unclipped the doorchain and pulled open the door.

'Thank you,' said Arnold, stepping into the flat. Drops of rainwater fell from his overcoat onto the worn carpet. He took Peter's hand and shook it firmly. 'My name, as I say, is Arnold Numan, and I'm from Kriger Investments.'

Peter sighed and said, 'I'm not interested in investments.'

'Ah!' said Arnold. 'Who is? Who is, Mr Voorjens? It's a terribly boring subject. But not one we should lightly dismiss. May I sit down?'

Arnold pushed himself into the room, unbuttoned his raincoat, and sat on Peter's saggy sofa. Peter closed the front door, wandered back to his chair and slowly lowered himself into it. Arnold opened his briefcase and removed a file full of papers. He sniffled a little as he did so.

'I think I'm coming down with a cold. It's the weather,' he said. He opened the file and flicked through it. 'Voorjens, Voorjens, Voorjens… Ah yes, Mr Voorjens. You have a company pension from…'

'Murit and Son,' said Peter.

'Murit and Son. Of course. The firm of solicitors.'

'Draughtsmen,' said Peter.

'Of course. And you're married?'

'My wife died eleven years ago,' said Peter.

'That's right. Let me tell you something, Mr Voorjens. Let me tell you something right from the off. I have something here. I have something here that you may well have absolutely no interest in. You may have no interest at all, and, if that is the case, then I will bid you a friendly farewell and leave and take this thing that I have to someone else. But I am going to show you it. You may well have no interest in what I am going to show you, but I am going to show you anyway.'

Arnold cleared away a memorabilia magazine and a television remote control from Peter's coffee table and placed them on the floor. Then he took a large laminated card from his briefcase. He opened the card and placed it on the table facing Peter. On it were pictures of coloured rocks.

'Do you know what they are, Mr Voorjens?' said Arnold, pointing at the card. 'They are precious stones. A diamond, a ruby, a sapphire, and that is an emerald. Why am I showing you these precious stones? Let me tell you. What is the number one thing a man desires when he reaches your age? Financial security? Wrong. He desires financial security for *his children*. His children and grandchildren. It's peace of mind, isn't it? When you are gone, you can be safe in the knowledge that your children will be looked after.'

'My children are fine,' said Peter.

'Do you know anything about investments, Mr Voorjens? I'm guessing you don't, but let me tell you this: Ninety-nine percent of all investments are a waste of time. This is because they rely on something called *the stock market*. We live in troubled times, Mr Voorjens. Everything fluctuates. We can rely on very little. We certainly cannot rely on the stock market. But what if there was an investment that relied on a solid commodity that *never loses value*? What if the value of this investment could rise but never fall? Take a look at the stones, Mr Voorjens.'

Arnold picked up the memorabilia magazine from the floor and began to thumb through it, the newsprint pages fluttering between his fingers. It contained advertisements, large picture ads and small text classifieds for military uniforms, guns and badges. Then he looked up and around the room, and spied the display case.

'You collect war memorabilia? Second World War? May I take a look? While you look at the stones?'

Arnold stood up from the sofa and walked over to the case. It was glass-fronted, and stood from the floor to the ceiling. Items were presented on shelves and hooks against a baize background. This was the hobby that Peter had taken up shortly after Stella's death.

'What I'm offering you, Mr Voorjens, is a chance to invest in a selection of premium precious stones,' said Arnold, poring over the display case. 'Our company has a secure facility in Switzerland containing over three thousand of the world's finest stones. What you're looking at there on your coffee table is... Jesus. Is this all real?'

'Yes,' said Peter. 'It's all real.'

Inside the case was an original SS uniform, cleaned and pressed, with peaked cap, grey jacket and trousers, and long black boots. It was complete with patches, badges, and sash, a metal swastika belt buckle, a leather holster, and a ceremonial dagger engraved with a message from Heinrich Himmler. Alongside it were framed propaganda posters, old photographs, original U-Boat and Panzer badges, and, the most prized of his possessions, a P-08 Luger. Every week Peter carefully stripped the pistol, first removing the magazine, then the takedown lever, next slipping off the side plate, then the barrel, the toggle, and the bolt. Each piece was carefully polished, the barrel was wiped with a cleaning rod, and the wooden grip was scrubbed with oil soap.

'May I take a closer look?' said Arnold. He pulled at the door of the display case.

'It's locked,' said Peter.

'Do you want to unlock it?' said Arnold. Then he saw the key was in the lock. He turned it, and pulled open the glass doors.

'Mr Numan, I don't want to invest in your diamonds,' said Peter.

Arnold reached into the case and pulled out the Luger.

'Mr Numan, thank you very much, but I'm not interested in your offer,' said Peter.

'This must be worth a fortune,' said Arnold, admiring the pistol. 'How much did you pay for it?'

'I didn't buy it,' said Peter, shifting in his seat.

'Isn't it illegal in our country to buy Nazi memorabilia, Mr Voorjens?'

'Please, Mr Numan,' said Peter, 'I don't mean any offence, but I'd like you to leave.'

'Don't worry, Mr Voorjens, I'll be leaving just as soon as we're finished here. Take a look at the stones.'

'I don't want to look at your stones.' Peter picked up the laminated card and placed it on top of Arnold's file. 'Please take your things and leave. I have things to do. And I'm expecting visitors any time now.'

Arnold ran his finger along the barrel of the pistol. He wiped away some rainwater that had run from his hair to his face.

'Mr Numan,' said Peter, 'I must insist that you leave right away.'

'You know, Mr Voorjens, I'm sure that the police would be very interested to hear about your little collection.'

'Please leave,' said Peter.

'What are you?' said Arnold. 'A bloody Nazi?'

The soldiers came in the spring of 1940. Dutch military resistance lasted five days. After that the soldiers marched into Amsterdam and stayed for almost five years. Peter lived through the Nazi occupation of Holland, but his father did not. Edward Voorjens was a tall, slim man who owned a printing press in the city. Many of his friends were Jews. Edward published the Joodse Weekblad for them.

At first, everything was the same. Soldiers in smart uniforms stood on street corners smoking cigarettes and laughing. Most were fearful of them, but some Dutch girls spoke to them and were given cigarettes. Then the Germans began to transport Jewish families to the East to find work. Neighbours disappeared without saying goodbye. The Davids lived right next door. Leanna David was due to be married in the spring. Over dinner, Peter's mother would ask him which of his friends were missing from school. He would tell her that Harold Sobel and George Pelski, and others from his class, had been absent for days. And she would cry. Then the Weekblad reported that the families had not been sent to find work. They had been sent to Buchenwald and Mauthausen, to Auschwitz and Sorbibor. Peter knew nothing of these places, but their names filled his mind with terror.

Peter last saw his father on a December evening in 1942. He watched him through a frosted windowpane as he walked along the cobbled street towards their home. He was smartly dressed, wearing a thick woollen coat over a suit, and carrying a brown paper parcel under his arm. Two SS officers stepped from a doorway and pushed Peter's father into a car. The car started away and was gone even before Peter could call for his mother. A city official said Edward Voorjens had been taken to Mauthausen. He never returned.

Peter and his mother spent the rest of the war claiming tiny victories against the Nazis. Peter would sell the soldiers lemonade made with urine. His mother would swap rationed foods with neighbours and cook forbidden feasts. They would write letters to Mauthausen and place the German stamp in the top left corner of the envelope, reserving the top right corner for the face of their own Queen Wilhelmina. Then, on Prince Bernard's birthday, the Dutch people took to the streets wearing orange carnations. Hundreds of them, holding hands, walked through the mist along the length of the canal as the Germans looked on.

And then it was all over. Peter stood in the snow on the pavement outside his mother's house as the Germans marched out. They no longer marched in time. One soldier broke rank and reached into his belt. He held out the Luger, and Peter took hold of the handle. The soldier's eyes were tired and watery beneath a creased brow. He offered a sad half-smile, like a defeated boxer. Then he turned to rejoin his unit. Peter felt the weight of the gun in his hand, and the soldiers marched around the corner of the street and were gone forever.

Arnold packed the file and laminated card into his briefcase and closed it at the clasp. 'I'm very sorry you're not interested in this investment. I must admit I feel I've wasted my time here. Perhaps my offer will be more suited to one of your neighbours. Do your neighbours know about your little collection, Mr Voorjens?'

'Please leave,' said Peter.

'I'll leave,' said Arnold. He fastened up his raincoat, picked up his briefcase, and stepped back to the display case. Peter watched as he picked up the Luger again. Arnold shut one eye, held the pistol up to his line of sight, and began to aim it variously around the room, at plant pots, at picture frames, at the television set. Then he stepped to the window and aimed the gun down into the puddled streets.

'Please, please leave,' said Peter.

'Or what?' said Arnold. 'You'll telephone the police? With this collection in your flat? This sick collection? Don't worry, Mr Voorjens, I'm leaving.' He stepped towards the door, the pistol still in his hand.

'Don't take the gun,' said Peter.

'*Don't take the gun?*' said Arnold, face reddening. 'Let me tell you something. I had grandparents who lived through the occupation of this city. Stood up against animals like you.' He pointed the gun at Peter's head. 'Do you know how many innocent people were taken from this city and killed? Thousands. More than ten thousand.' He began to spit. 'Ten, fifteen thousand people. You sick…'

Arnold's breathing quickened, and saliva bubbled at his lips. At the end of his outstretched arm his right index finger trembled over the trigger of the Luger.

Then Peter stared into the barrel of the gun and spoke. 'I have a friend who keeps snakes,' he said. 'Poisonous snakes. He has been bitten twice, and almost died. But he won't give up his collection. I hate the Luger, the uniform, and everything else I have collected. But I can't allow you to take it from me.'

Arnold's grip tightened around the pistol, and he took a deep breath. For a moment the two men listened to the rain tapping on the windowpane.

Then Arnold said, 'You Nazi bastard,' and pulled the trigger.

The gun clicked harmlessly. Neither man said anything. Arnold released a long exhale, and threw the Luger onto the sofa. He turned, opened the front door, and stepped out into the stairwell, pulling the door behind him.

Peter sat for a short while listening to the rain. The breeze made it roll as it fell. Then he gripped the arms of his chair and raised himself to his feet. He stood for a moment and straightened himself out. The electric fire made a clicking noise and the bars glowed red. He picked up the Luger and carried it to the display case. Taking a cloth from the case, he polished the barrel, the body, and the grip. He replaced the pistol, ran his hand over the SS uniform, and carefully closed the case. Through the walls of the flat he heard a neighbour playing piano music. Then he went back to his chair, sat down, and looked out of the window.

Two children were playing in puddles by the canal. There was blue sky in the distance. Soon the rain would stop.

THE CURIOUS ANATOMY OF BROTHER WINTON

by SAM MORRIS

A STORY IN THREE PARTS BY MAURICE THE MONK
(TEMPORARILY EXCOMMUNICATED)

1. MY BROTHER - A LARGE MAN INDEED

FOR a big man, my brother had exceptionally small feet. I couldn't help but wonder at them as he shared the very next bunk next to mine in the main dormitory. Every morning, through half closed eyes, I would see these tiny feet emerge from under the blankets. Every morning I would wonder for a second, in my still dreamlike state, if they weren't the feet of a beautiful young woman. As I wondered this I would feel a guilt welling up from within me and was visited by the most unbecoming thoughts. I am not sure if I was more relieved or disappointed when these beautiful and dainty little feet were followed out from under the blankets by the enormous and cumbersome bulk of Brother Winton.

He was easily the largest monk at our Monastery, towering over the rest of us in his oversized cassock. This fashioned from two ordinary ones and bound together with course thread. In the early morning light, on our way to worship Prime, he cast a shadow that stretched all the way from the door of our Dormitory to the steps of our beloved church. My own barely reached half that distance. Regardless his large and uncouth size, I would doubt whether a more devout or gentler man ever graced this earth. He hardly uttered a word to anyone, even though he is under no oath. He held his large body with the most poignant meekness. His large shoulders hunched and his head turned down to the ground.

Once, when I had to rouse him from prayer, doing so by the customary method of laying a soft hand on his shoulder and whispering into his ear so as to not disturb the others, I gave him such a shock that he leapt up to his feet with alarm. Thus sending me first upwards several feet into the air, and then crashing backwards several yards into the first of the wooden pews. I would have liked to have been angry at him, but he looked so very, very sorry. Mumbling a continuous apology, the words tumbling over each other, he picked me gently up into his arms and carried me all the way to the infirmary. This being about three hundred yards away, in the fragrant shadow of the grand stables and the less than grand pigsties. He carried me the entire distance in one go, and in one hand. Praise be the Lord's mercy!

As he carried me thus, I kept meaning to ask him my question. Frustratingly, each time as I was about to come out with it, I would hold back, thinking that perhaps there was a better way to phrase it, or that this was not quite the right time. Catching the words a fraction before they left my mouth I emitted a noise that must have sounded like an enfeebled simpering. It certainly served to send Brother Winton towards the infirmary with even greater haste. Before I had adequate chance for my question I found myself gently ensconced in a straw bed and being tended by several of the younger novices.

For some weeks previous I had been meaning to ask Brother Winton my question. Unfortunately it was, as you will see, of a rather delicate nature. It would not have been easy to approach a good friend with such a request; let alone a lonely soul who weighed at least two of me. You see, my question may have appeared a little, well, crude. That is to say, to the untutored ear, it my have sounded like the kind of speculation indulged only by the unholy, the foolish or the drunk. Nothing, as you shall see, can have been further from the truth.

As is not at all unusual, and in order I keep myself occupied during my days at the monastery, I had decided to indulge myself in some studies of a scientific nature. This was not the sort of science concerned with alchemy, necromancy or other such devilry. It concerned simply the order of nature, and rather more specifically it concerned both the essence and the anatomy of a man. Now, as you will see this was a study of no little importance to a devout holy man, like myself. Beyond any serious doubt it concerned the wonderment of creation on this very earth, by our Lord above us in Heaven – praise be his ingenuity!

As I am sure you are aware the Aedificium of our great monastery boasts one of the largest collections of texts in the Christian world. There were books concerning every subject imaginable, both of devout pursuits and concerning many other fields of interest. Some of these books were more than a little controversial. Some a direct contradiction to our word of the Lord. Nonetheless, it was our wise and distinguished Abbot's opinion that one must know the Devil as well as the Lord, in order to distinguish clearly between the two. Therefore, even more junior monks like myself were allowed access to some interesting books. Books that many monks, at other lesser monasteries, would not be bid the great fortune to peruse.

It is in my inspection of such books that I have been able to come to some fascinating insights about the nature of man. Even if most of the inferences in many of those more controversial books were brazenly untrue, and no doubt inspired of the devil, a diligent scholar could impart some very useful information still, from such tomes. During these studies I became absorbed in one particular idea. This was based in both the area of modern science and was in addition abundant in the glory of our Lord – praise be his magnificence!

In short, and without cause for needless preamble, it is my firm belief that one is able to fully assay the character and substance of a man, and perhaps even more besides, by the measurement of his physical characteristics alone. I shall not impart you all the specifics here. As this is not the principal concern of my tale. However, in order I state my interests more clearly; I will give you token example of my theories:

It is true that, of the many things about a man you can tell from appearance alone, one is his base intelligence. By this I do not mean how much he knows of the scriptures, or the teachings of our Lord. But instead you may tell his cunning and his ability to solve the novel problems that we are all confronted with from time to time. I have, in the course of my study, deduced the main way you may measure such characteristic. This is done by careful observation of the size of the subject's ears or the nose. A smaller set of ears and nose denote a rather limited intellect, and little capacity for deeper thinking. Whilst larger specimens of these two organs denote a person of higher, and indeed deeper intellect. Safe to say, although it renders me rather unattractive, I have somewhat large ears. In addition to these aural adornments I possess the most wondrously outsized beak of a nose in the whole of the monastery, if not the whole of Christendom. You must understand that, rather than making feel me in any way superior to my Brothers, this blessing makes me more convinced of the accuracy of my work, its importance to the advancement of mankind, and of course too the glory of our Lord – praise be his shrewdness!

This example brings me, I hope, rather neatly to another thing you may tell of a man by his physical appearance alone. Using my methods you may accurately gauge his temperament and more specifically his level of physical and moral aggression. This, as you will see, brings us by increments closer to my interest in the size of Brother Winton's feet, all of which shall be explained in due course. For now I will simply say that, rather unfortunately, the actual organ that determines the temperament of a man is none other than the penis.

2. PRAISE BE – A PLAN!

Now, it most obviously unusual, needless for me to say, to make acquaintance with a man's penis before you make fuller acquaintance of his personality and temperament. You may indeed get to know a fellow most intimately without ever having need to spy the contents of his undergarments. This, I at first feared, may render my method of assaying the temperament of a man rather impractical. That was, until I came upon a rather novel solution, praise be to my large ears and magnificent nose!

In my readings at the Aedificium one day I came by chance upon a rather interesting tome. It concerned the voyage of a certain botanist who, in partaking of a journey across a variety of tropical islands, reported most usefully not only what he found in simple material terms, but what may be derived and learnt by such discoveries. By careful study of all the strange and magnificent creatures discovered, the author found cause to draw some interesting conclusions as to the anatomy of all living creatures. I shall, of course, impart you an example, this being most relevant to this tale: It told of how you may tell the size of a bird's beak by the length of its clawed feet; no matter the size of the rest of the bird's body. Without lengthy discussion of my precise reasoning, in summary, by this very rational, I was able to venture that you may be able to tell the size of a man's penis by the size of his feet. Therefore determining his temperament, without need for becoming far more acquainted with the man in question than is proper and correct for a man of my calling.

Now, those amongst you larger of ear or more magnificent of nose may already be able to deduce my interest in my Brother

Winton, and why I considered him such an opportune trial for my theory. For if correct, despite him being very large of body, he should have the very humblest of penises. I am only a little ashamed to admit that I indulged myself by imagining it to be more little more than a small bean in a thick leathery sack; shrivelled and very, very tiny, in contrast to the full organ of a man such as myself. However, I had cause to remind myself I must first find a means of discovering if this assumption were true, before becoming too carried away by its brilliance. Such is the nature of scientific forms of study.

My first impulse was simply to enquire of my Brother his exact dimensions. This rather frustratingly proved more difficult than I had first hoped. How exactly one was to put such delicate a question was never entirely clear to me. Each variation that I imagined was either too direct and likely to offend. Or, conversely, was too obscure and likely to be met with bewilderment. The longer I left this question hanging, unanswered, the more I became engaged by it. Rehearsing lines over and over in my head, and all the time wondering at the precise length and nature of my Brother Winton's manhood.

This may sound an unseemly pursuit for a devout man like myself. In light of this, and in defence if such were necessary - I would say to you that you must consider all the factors pertinent to my interests. On the first hand the goals of my inquiry were of the humblest and most noble origins. Pertaining to the ordering and understanding of the wonderful ingenuity of our Lord in Heaven. In addition, I will admit it is true; monastic life is rather frugal in engaging diversions, other than those of a religious or theological nature of course. It is only to be expected that at times the mind must wander off the natural course of things. In order to consider the beauty, and indeed the mystery of this magnificent Earth created by our Lord in Heaven! I say this not to excuse what followed, but rather to engage an understanding of those events that subsequently came to pass. So that perhaps you may think a little more kindly upon me.

As shall be fully imparted, I decided the only sure way to discover the length of my Brother's manhood was to descry myself, in secret of course, the exact nature of the organ in question. In using the mental faculties that I have been blessed with I came upon a rather ingenious and inventive solution, Lord forgive me my vanity! You see, Brother Winton had a rather strange habit that the Abbot seemed only too happy to indulge him in. It was known to the even the lowliest of novices that every Sunday, after Matins, he would retire to room below the bell tower, above the entrance to the church, and flail himself. He did this, so it is believed, to atone for the sins he had committed previous to entering our sanctum. What these sins were I had not the slightest notion. Rumour has is that he is covered all over in some strange scars, and speaks very little of his past beyond the walls of the monastery. Some speculate that he was a heathen solider that killed many a Christian warrior, before he saw the light and gave himself to the service of our Lord. Such idle gossip is of course of little interest to the scientific mind. Of most interest to me was that he did this flailing completely naked, and whilst the bells were being rung in the tower above him.

The top of the room in which he performed his flagellation had, at its very summit, a small hole. The purpose of this hole to allow the pull cords for the mighty bells ringing above to travel downwards without impediment. An enquiring mind like my own would naturally note that this opening was, by a fraction, large enough for a smaller man such as myself to fit through. Without further ado the essence of my plan was thus. I would suspend myself by one of these cords, in order that I might descend into the chamber for a brief second, regard the object of my mission, and then disappear back out the way I had come.

The difficult part of my plan was to find a reason to be in the vicinity of the bell tower, after the ceremony of Matins had finished. This is where my true stroke of genius lay. As a monk it is only customary to partake in regular confession. It is one of the few privileges of our calling; that we are able to report our sins at virtually any hour of the day. At such an early hour in the morning all the senior members of the monastery would be busy, with their individual preparations for the day ahead. It was my hope that at this hour of the morning the listener to my confession would be none other than Brother Mathews. Dear Brother Matthews! A kindly and devout man of great and advancing years. Easily was he the oldest of all those living in our community. In those few other occasions I'd had my confessions with him, he had been sound asleep only a few minutes after I had begun. My plan was to therefore sneak out of the wooden confession chamber whilst the old man slept and engage the rest of my plan. It would not be long before I was back in the chamber, where I could awake my Brother with a loud cough, as has become the custom when you are at confession with Brother Matthews. Of course, despite the very best of plans, often things do not turn out exactly as they are envisioned.

3. THE BELL TOWER

On the morning of my exploit I thought it prudent to calm my nerves using some of the herbs that had been given to me in the infirmary, after Brother Winton had sent me tumbling into the air. In the infirmary these herbs had proved extraordinarily effective. They were able to reduce my pain greatly and induce me into a state of great relaxation. In this peaceful state my imagination was free to wander as it pleased. I was able to behold the most amazing visions. The visions I partook of being perhaps worthy of a saint, far be in from me, a humble monk, to indulge in such speculation. That said, perhaps on the morning in question, in hindsight, the consumption of this herb was not the wisest course of action.

As I made my way across the brown sods of bare earth towards the church very early that very morn, the gusts of wind had a rather unusual effect on me. As they swirled in the few strands of hardy and wild grass that dotted the ground I fancied I could discern a being of some kind skittering around me. These same gusts of wind billowed my cassock around me and I fancied that this being, whatever it may be, was pushing and nudging me with some nefarious intent. This made me feel quite pale, and I am ashamed to admit, a little afraid, as I stumbled in the early morning gloom. Due most likely to this fear the moaning of this wind across the stone eaves of the church began to sound like a chorus of mournful and bedevilled voices; whispering, whispering, into my ear. The voices imparting to me the strangest of notions, of which I shall not utter here.

As may be imagined, I was more than a little relieved when I entered the light and the sanctity of the church. Once the ceremony had begun I started to feel much, much better. I sung with a much greater degree of heart that I would normally have done, especially at such an early hour. I caught a few bemused glances from my Brothers around me, but I cared not, such was the state of my elation. During the sermon I became unusually captivated by the stained glass windows, discovering many strange and beguiling patterns of light in them that had not struck me before. Where shards of many different colours meet each other and seemed to dance and shimmer as they overlapped, creating new and dazzling patterns as I watched. All the while the Abbots voice filled the vast cavernous space of the church, in a multitude of tiny but perfect echoes – praise be indeed to the glory of our Lord!

After the ceremony, in very fine spirits indeed, I put into play the first step of my plan. On entering the low and cramped space of the confession box I was met with the sight of many long, grey stands of beard reaching at me through the grill. Being in such high spirits I tugged at them and said, 'Wake up Brother Matthews, I have some wonderful confessions to make.' He was a little startled and started muttering, the sound muffled by those same silver strands. I nonetheless started my confession un-heeded saying whatever happened to appear in my mind.

I will admit it always struck me as a little odd; the frequency with which we monks were expected to each confess our sins. That is not to say that I never did commit such acts as warranted forgiveness in the eyes of our Lord. But you understand, living as I did amongst the holy and devout, the occasions for unholy thoughts, let alone deeds, were really rather slim. It was for this reason I began to invent some prolonged fabrication of how I had been coveting another brother's portion of raw beans, last Tuesday at Vespers. In addition I told of how I had caught myself wondering that the wooden bunk of my Brother Finnit, sleeping next to me on the other side from Brother Winton, may be longer and wider than my own. I even ventured that it looked as if it was made from softer wood, so being relatively speaking a little more comfortable.

In my relaxed state from the herbs I had consumed, I let my voice do the wandering in that confined space. The more I spoke the more I began to feel a little detached from my own oration. As if I were able to sit back a little and listen to myself talk as you are doing now. As I listened to myself I began to hear alongside my own voice a background noise that I had not noticed before; a kind of roaring wailing sound. After a time I began to fancy I could hear mighty storm cutting across the earth outside. I found myself begin to imagine an angry torrent of rain that lashed down upon all of us. Truly biblical volumes of water that fell from the sky above us, onto the roof of confession box itself rather than on the church, which even at the time seemed rather strange. I imagined this downpour to have been happening for some days now passed. So that it caused all the surrounding rivers and lakes to burst their banks, and as they did so merge with the seas at the edge of the land. I fancied that myself, and Brother Mathews of course, were set afloat in our small wooden craft – the confession box no less. The two of us drifting away atop a mighty ocean that now had covered the entirety of God's Earth.

Floating on this mighty body of water, I started to hear the most wondrous sound; a low, sonorous bellow that vibrated our entire craft with its power. I immediately supposed this to be the song of a whale. A mighty beast, hundreds of times the size of a man, that lives in the oceans according to the books I have studied in the Aedificium. I was so enchanted by the deep melodies of this beast that I decided to step outside the craft, to see if I couldn't spot the creature, beneath the deep blue waves of the endless ocean.

On opening my eyes, as you may imagine, I found myself back in the confessional box, in the corner of the nave, with Brother Mathew's snores sending tremors through our enclosure. I was a little confused at this turn of events at first, but then remembered the important quest which I had entrusted myself with. I thanked the Lord for my good fortune, and stumbling a little as I exited the confession box I tried to dismiss the notion that the entire world was covered in briny, turbulent waters.

In sneaking upwards, to the room in the bell tower above Brother Winton, I was fortunate to meet no other souls wandering in the Church. I could hear the bells above me, and knew the peal that was being played on those mighty instruments only too well. Having in the past, some years ago now, been one of the bell pullers. I was able to judge that one of the cords, that was presently still, would shortly be pulled again. Wasting no time I quickly attached this rope to my ankle and awaited my cord be tugged. As hoped, in short time I was aloft in the air. Rising slowly at first I fancied that I heard some laboured breathing and cries of mild alarm coming from above me, but paying this no heed. After eventually reaching my summit downwards I plummeted. Towards the opening to the room below and the target of my curiosity!

I shot through that narrow opening and descended rapidly into the darkened chamber below. Descending so swiftly it took me some moments to get my bearings and discover the whereabouts of Brother Winton in relation to myself. It was a mighty surprised when I did.

For I blush to tell you now that Bother Winton was in apparent possession of the largest male member imaginable. Even given his great size it was an extraordinary large appendage. I feared that were he to wade through a patch of stinging weed in a loose cassock, as is customary, he would render himself insensible with the stings he might receive. It was of such a staggering girth and length that I felt the need to cross myself as I ascended back into the chamber above. This turned out to be a rather unfortunate mistake. For in crossing myself I extended the width of my body, and duly came into crashing and painful contact with the surround of the narrow hole in the ceiling. Thus causing me to come to a shuddering halt. In my complete surprise at this turn of events, and with Brother Winton now looking mournfully upwards to my position, I began to say the most random of things. The herbs no doubt taking their part in my utterings.

'It's very clement outside,' I said as I slowly descended.

Then, a little further down, I said, 'Fried herrings for supper is without doubt my favourite meal.'

It was deeply unfortunate for all concerned that, as I came to a stop directly before the bemused and rather fearful looking Brother Winton, and with him stopped with his flailing twig now raised above me, and with my own genitals revealed as my cassock rode down over my head, that the Abbot should choose to pay this room a visit. What made it all the more unfortunate was the fact that our wise leader was engaged in showing a small group of novice candidates around the monastery. With my cassock over my head and oblivious to our recent arrivals I continued to spout utter nonsense, mistaking the shrill screaming to be coming from Brother Winton, rather than some very shocked boys from the local town. I honestly hoped that I might calm him a little with my words.

'You have a marvellous penis my good Brother,' I said, 'Proof of the wonderment of our Lord in Heaven I have no doubt.'

Alas, what a truly regrettable incident! To his credit the Ab-

bot, after a prolonged chastisement of my character and suitabil-
ity to the calling, offered me a position in the outer sections of
the monastery. This would of course be as a lowly labourer, and
not as a fellow monk. I would man the main gate and in addition
tend to the pigs and other animals. Admittedly, I did give it a
moment's consideration, but decided that it simply could not be.
How could I stay after such an incident? I would never be held
with any respect and worse still would be forbidden entry to my
beloved Aedificium. It was with some sadness that I decided I
should take my leave, by cover of the night, directly after this
most sad of days. I have told myself ever since how this incident
might opportune me to explore the world and refine my theories,
for the benefit of science and for mankind. But 'tis lonely and
long the path that I tread. So be it and least I forget; praise be to
the Lord and his strange but divine ways!

This, I am sure you are relieved, concludes my sorry tale.
Please, I would beg of you, after being so kind as to hear my
story, take pity on a poor but pious man. I can tell by your large,
and may I say rather deep and beautiful eyes that you are a
generous and undoubtedly a very thoughtful person. All I ask is
enough money for some food, and perchance a bed for the night.
And I thank again you for listening to my tale. God be with you
and – praise be to the mystery and the glory of our Lord! Amen.

THE SLUG
by BERNARD LANDRETH

WHEN Ambrose switched on his living room light in the early hours of one morning to discover a slug on the carpet, his surprise led him, not to step back in revulsion, but to sink to his knees in fascination. He had never had a garden and never had cause to think of slugs as pests. The general perception of them as dirty, black, slimy creatures was the motivation behind one of his more disgusting pranks as a schoolboy, some forty years previously. He would bite the end off a liquorice stick, suck it until it was moist with spit and then pretend to find it in a flowerbed and pop it into his mouth.

The slug he saw on the carpet, halfway between his sofa and his front door, was not at all disgusting in appearance. It was around two inches long, sleek, and glistened in the colour of Cotswold stone. It tapered elegantly at each end and had an unusual texture with hundreds of minute dimples between which moisture was causing the glistening effect. On its head were two sets of antennae, the longer pair moving around independently of each other, as if they were searching for something.

Apart from the slight movement of its antennae, the slug was motionless, presumably disoriented by the sudden light. It appeared to have been heading in the direction of the front door. A narrow trail behind it, hardly noticeable against the faded blue carpet, indicated that it had come from behind the sofa. He noticed other silvery ribbons leading between the sofa and the door, which opened from the street directly into the room. There was a small gap between the door jamb and the skirting board which was at right angles to it, from which the trails seemed to emanate.

As Ambrose watched, the slug began to slowly move towards the door. He found this interesting. A cartoon slug would have arched its back, bringing its rear end forward, then stretched its head and the front portion of its body forward by an equal amount. That is how he would have imagined that a slug would move – in a series of constrictions and extensions. But this slug was sliding forward effortlessly. It was graceful. It was... Ambrose stopped short of the word beautiful, then decided that it was the only word to use.

Ambrose didn't like having to rely on words. This was one of the worst things about not having had a drink. Without drink, he seemed to need words to access his mind, and there were only a finite number of words available to him to express an infinite number of experiences and emotions. Having to think in words was limiting. It could result in frustration; it could make him feel ignorant, or ridiculous when ascribing a word like beautiful to a slug. After a few drinks, a direct link was established between his mind and his consciousness. He no longer had to express to himself what he was thinking or feeling – he knew.

He had not had a drink since lunchtime. The evening had dragged, the night had been even worse, and now, this early morning, he felt wide awake. There were still five hours to wait until his appointment at the doctor.

He had made the mistake, several years previously, of answering his doctor honestly when asked about his drinking.

'Four or five pints a day', he had said.

The doctor had written: *Very heavy drinker* on his medical records, which Ambrose thought was misleading. He knew men who would drink that amount at lunchtime. As his drinking had intensified, the amount he admitted to on his infrequent appointments reduced.

'Never more than a couple of pints.'

'A pint or two a couple of times a week.'

'An occasional glass of wine.'

And he always made sure that he was free from alcohol before the appointment, in case a blood test should be needed.

And so it was that Ambrose was sober, in the early hours of the morning, watching a beautiful slug moving across his carpet.

He could have easily picked it up with a tissue and thrown it out into the road, or squashed it, or flushed it down the toilet. But the experience was so unusual and slug was so graceful that it would have seemed wrong to do that.

He looked around his living room – half a dozen empty lager cans filled the waste paper basket, several back copies of *The Sun* lay on the floor, and a dinner plate on the coffee table had the residues baked beans and brown sauce hardening on it. He could hear his lodger – the perpetrator of the mess – snoring heavily upstairs, a sound that had contributed to his sleepless night.

The slug was moving slowly towards the door – small and silent – leaving only a pretty little silvery thread in its wake. Switching off the light, Ambrose climbed the stairs with a determination that was alien to his normally placid nature and walked into his lodger's room to shake him roughly. The snoring ceased abruptly, to be followed by a grunt and a stream of inarticulate curses.

'Shut up,' said Ambrose firmly, before returning to his bedroom.

Ambrose had many reasons for regretting taking in a lodger.

When they had met, Jed told him that he had just been thrown out by a woman with whom he had been sharing a flat. He was sitting at a bar with a large rucksack and two black plastic bin-liners that appeared to contain everything he owned. Ambrose was impressed by his relaxed attitude to his situation. He seemed friendly, he had bought Ambrose a pint, which led to another, then another, and the day had ended with him taking Jed home and installing him in his spare room.

The following morning he had cursed his stupidity.

For the first few weeks Jed had paid his rent promptly, and treated Ambrose and his house with a degree of respect, but lately there had been a noticeable lack of respect and rent. Jed had started to act as if he had equal rights over the house and all its contents – especially the food and drink. Ambrose had been forced to move his stock of vodka to the wardrobe in his bedroom. Jed had also started to invite rather loud and aggressive acquaintances around, and had developed the habit of referring to Ambrose as 'Bro', a name he appeared to find amusing every time he used it.

'Bro!' he would shout out if he met Ambrose during the day.

'This is Bro, my landlord,' he would announce when he re-turning home with one or more of his drinking companions. 'You can crash here. Bro won't mind. Good man, Bro. The best.'

'Don't worry about it, Bro,' had become his response to all complaints or requests for rent.

Like Ambrose, Jed's life revolved around alcohol, but that was all that they had in common. Ambrose had sunk slowly and undramatically into alcoholism over a period of thirty years. He used alcohol in a controlled manner rather as a medication.

Before Jed moved in, his typical day would start with a tumbler of vodka and orange juice in equal proportions followed by breakfast. He would then walk into town and spend the morning either reading in the library or sitting in the park. He would return home for lunch – another glass of vodka with a cheese sandwich – after which he would read his latest library book or doze for a couple of hours, depending how well he had slept the night before. For dinner he would cook a vegetable soup or pasta with sauce out of a tin. He would then spend the evening with the remainder of his daily bottle of vodka, watching television or listening to Classic FM on the radio.

On Mondays he would have lunch in the Joiner's Arms – just off the High Street, on Thursdays he would shop and on Sundays he would postpone his first drink until he returned from morning service at the local parish church.

His lodger, around twenty years his junior, did not have this discipline. He was erratic and uneconomical in his use of alcohol. He would drink anything at any time. He would spend as much on three pints of lager in a town centre pub as Ambrose would on the bottle of cheap vodka that would last him the whole day. Sometimes he would binge to the point of coma, after which he would pledge to reform and remain sober for periods of a up to week. During these periods of sobriety he would formulate elaborate plans that were completely unachievable and the realisation of this would force him back to the pub.

If his use of alcohol was unpredictable, Jed's personal hygiene was consistently poor – drunk or sober. His hair was dark, shoulder-length, unwashed and oily. He did not appear to use the bathroom other than as a toilet, and the feeling that he never even washed his hands had prompted Ambrose to keep his toothbrush and more personal toiletries in a sponge bag in his bedroom. He had only one pair of jeans, which were originally blue denim but now appeared smooth and black with wear and dirt. The filthy state of his jeans was highlighted by his shiny leather jacket, slightly too small for him, which appeared to be almost new – Ambrose was convinced that he must have stolen it. Beneath the jacket he would wear an off-white t-shirt.

In addition to being distasteful, Jed's presence had begun to seriously upset Ambrose's routine. If Jed appeared to be stopping in the house, Ambrose would either retire to his bedroom or go out. He now avoided the Joiner's Arms, his favourite pub, because Jed had started to drink there. If Jed was around at dinner time, Ambrose would buy a bag of chips rather than cook.

Jed was at his worst when his abstinence was caused by lack of money. At such times he would either become morose and seek to engage Ambrose in self-pitying conversations about the meaning of life, or embark on periods of manic activity, both of which Ambrose found quite disturbing.

It was on one such evening that Jed began to vacuum the house, muttering about the state it was in. The house was in a mess, largely of his own making, and Ambrose wished that he would direct his attention to his personal cleanliness. Jed insisted that Ambrose vacate the sofa on which he was watching television. The lodger's mood was not improved by the sight of his landlord drinking vodka and the knowledge that he was not going to be offered a drink. As he pulled the sofa away from the wall, numerous silvery trails were revealed, like strands of tinsel on the carpet. The trails were interwoven into a maze, reminding Ambrose of a child's puzzle in which one has to follow a line through a tangle of other lines.

'That's snails, man, or fucking slugs or something,' Jed had cried out in disgust.

'More likely a slug,' replied Ambrose calmly. After his recent encounter he had been noticing new trails each morning and had removed them by rubbing his foot on the carpet on his way into town. He had never thought to look under the sofa.

'What are you going to do about it?'

'What do you expect me to do about it?' asked Ambrose.

'Slugs, man! It's unhygienic – it's a health hazard.'

'It's not a health hazard. Give me that Hoover,' Ambrose replied. He took the brush attachment off the tube, switched on the old cylinder vacuum cleaner and quickly removed all traces of the delicate trail. 'There, no problem,' he concluded as he pushed the sofa back against the wall and stretched out on it.

His lodger was in no mood to let the matter rest. 'You can't have slugs crawling around your house. For fuck's sake man, it's… it's…' his voice tailed off in disbelief.

'So catch them and throw them out. Or get out yourself. Find some other idiot who'll put up with you for forty quid a week.' Ambrose was attempting to appear relaxed on the sofa, but as he looked up at his lodger, he felt that he was in danger of losing control of the situation.

He slept very little that night. As well as being younger than him, Jed was several inches taller and several stones heavier. He realised that if his lodger continued to refuse to pay his rent, there was little he could do about it.

The next day started badly. Ambrose had been drinking through the night. He ate some toast and then returned to bed to sleep through until lunchtime. Waking with a sense of disorientation and anger at the disturbance to his routine, he walked into town without eating lunch and without noticing the darkening sky. He was wearing a lightweight jacket and had not taken the large umbrella he usually carried if he thought there was even the slightest risk of rain.

In town he visited the library and sat down with a large reference book on property law. He found a section dealing with tenancy but it was written in legal terms that he found difficult to understand. As he read his concentration was interrupted by the sudden onset of very heavy rain, pounding on the roof light above the table at which he was sitting. He looked up to see a thunder-dark sky through the rain-washed glass. His head began to ache – he needed a drink. He went to stand in the doorway of the library as the rain continued to pound the pavements and run in small torrents down the channels on each side of the carriageway. Removing his jacket to drape it over his head, he made a sudden run for a café bar across the road, where he spent the next two hours and ten pounds that he could not afford on four small bottles of strong, expensive lager.

He walked home through a light rain along streets running with water. Opening his front door he found his lodger, reclining on the sofa with a glass in his hand and a bottle of vodka, less than half full, on the coffee table. It was a bottle of Ambrose's vodka – a bottle that he must have taken from the wardrobe in Ambrose's bedroom. Next to the vodka was a large plastic container of table salt, the little chute on its lid raised. Jed looked up at him. He was drunk, and seemed to be wildly triumphant.

'I got the slugs – three of the bastards!' he exclaimed enthusiastically, then noticing Ambrose staring at the vodka, added, 'I'll pay for the booze, Bro.'

He rose from the sofa as he said it and grabbing Ambrose roughly by the arm, pulled him into the street. The pavement was still very wet. He pointed down to where it abutted with the front wall of the house.

'Three bastard slugs! I salted 'em.' He beamed at Ambrose and then started to dance on the wet slabs. 'Salted slugs! Salted slugs! Get your salted slugs here!' he shouted. A face appeared at a window across the street.

Along the frontage of his small terraced house – no more than fifteen feet in length – Ambrose could see a sprinkling of salt and three slugs in their death throes. The rain must have bought them out to meet a fate for which evolution had not prepared them. The smallest was dark brown, about an inch in length; another, slightly longer, was blackish, and closest to the door, the largest one – ochre in colour – was arched grotesquely in a huge smear of mucus, its life fluid being sucked out of it. Ambrose stared at it, appalled, then turned away. His lodger had stopped dancing and was grinning. Ambrose hit him, full in the face, with all his strength.

Jed fell backwards to sit on the wet pavement for a few seconds, the triumph on his face replaced by that expression of bewilderment that drunks wear when faced with the unexpected. He put his hand to his face and then examined the blood on it.

'Fuck,' he muttered to himself, then repeated it before looking up at Ambrose. 'They're slugs, man. They're bastard slugs.'

Ambrose thought about making a dash for the door and locking it behind him. Instead, he stood his ground. 'Don't worry about the rent, just get your stuff, give me the key, and get out.'

Jed raised himself slowly from the pavement, and for a moment Ambrose thought he was going to do as he had been told. But then he launched himself forward, clutching Ambrose around the waist and bringing him crashing against the next door neighbour's front door. They struggled on the pavement for sometime, the blood from Jed's face becoming smeared over both their shirts. Ambrose was trying to keep Jed on the ground, but after a couple of minutes the difference in age, size and weight began to take effect, and by the time the police arrived Jed had him by the throat up against the neighbour's red transit van.

They were taken to the police station in separate vehicles. On arrival Ambrose could hear Jed's voice, still screaming about slugs. When Ambrose was interviewed he explained that the argument had been about non-payment of rent. He was polite and apologetic, explaining that they had both had a bit too much to drink. All he said about Jed was that he was a strange man with some unusual problems. The constable who interviewed him returned a few minutes later.

'Your lodger seems quite distressed about some slugs,' he said.

Ambrose tapped his forehead. 'He's a bit crazy actually. He's obsessed with them. I think he thinks I'm breeding them to attack him while he's asleep.' He shook his head. 'It's the drink.'

The young constable made a note and then grinned. 'He's more than a bit crazy. I wouldn't want to share a house with him.'

Ambrose was cautioned and allowed to go home. The constable and the duty sergeant were both quite sympathetic. They told him that his lodger would be kept in the cells overnight.

Arriving home late in the evening, Ambrose went straight to his room, drank a mug full of neat vodka, lay on his bed, and surprisingly, fell asleep. He woke early with a feeling of foreboding. There was no going back from the situation that had arisen the previous evening. Ambrose checked his spare room. Jed was not in the house, but his belongings were still there.

He ate his breakfast toast with his early morning drink and walked into town earlier than usual. He did not want to be at home when Jed returned. He spent a couple of hours in the library, but could not face the prospect of tenancy law books so he flicked through various magazines without being able to concentrate. The events of the previous evening were still sharp in his mind – the fight, Jed drinking his vodka, the police station, and as vivid as any of them, the dying, ochre-coloured slug. He started to feel slightly sick and left the library.

It was eleven o'clock. He walked past the café bar he had visited the day before, past the Joiner's Arms, to the Station Hotel, where he drank two pints of bitter before noon. He ordered a third, which he promised himself he would make last for at least an hour. 'Bad habits,' he muttered to himself.

Just before one o'clock he walked home and quietly let himself in. The house was still empty, and Jed's gear was still in the spare room. He could imagine him in town, getting more and more drunk before staggering back. He immediately wanted to go out again. He made a cheese sandwich, which he ate hurriedly, then poured half a bottle of vodka into a small flask and walked down to the park.

After the deluge of the previous day it was a pleasantly sunny. He sat on a bench, opened his flask and filled the small cup. 'Bastard,' he muttered, then aware of what he had just done, repeated, 'Bastard. Bastard.'

He looked around. No one had heard him. He shook his head. He was breaking all his own rules – all the criteria he had set himself to avoid ever becoming a drunk. He was exceeding his daily allowance of alcohol, drinking alone in pubs, drinking in the park and worse of all, he had started swearing and muttering to himself. 'Bastard,' he muttered again.

He sipped from the cup. He felt like stretching out the bench and trying to sleep but that would be even worse than drinking and muttering. Instead he began to walk through the park, sitting at various points to take a drink from his flask. By the time it was empty he had been around the park several times and it was getting dark.

He walked home slowly. His house was in darkness. The curtains to the front room were open to reveal an unlit interior. He opened the door and switched on the light. His lodger was lying on the sofa. A glass lay on the floor with a second empty bottle of Ambrose's vodka next to it. Jed lay on his side, still and dark. His jeans – wet with urine – shone to match the blackness of his leather jacket. The only skin visible was part of his face beneath the thick, greasy hair. It was pallid and moist with sweat. A small quantity of vomit had dribbled from his mouth to stain the sofa. The one eye which was visible was closed.

Ambrose bent to touch the shoulder and shake it, then withdrew his hand from the coldness and texture of the leather, and the stillness of the body. He could not see or hear any sign of breathing. He raised his foot to the shoulder and rocked the body again. There was a slight jerk and a sound rather like a hiccup. The eyelid opened to reveal a bloodshot white of the eye. Only the bottom part of the pupil was visible and this seemed to be staring upwards into the skull.

Ambrose picked up the empty vodka bottle, held it upside down, and watched the last few residual drops trickle down the inside of the glass and on to the carpet. He placed the bottle on the coffee table, noticing as he did so the container of salt which still stood there from the previous night. He picked it up, considered pouring the remaining contents over the lump on his sofa, but decided against it. It would have no effect and would be difficult to explain.

Switching off the light, he stepped back out on to the street and began walking into town. He stopped under a streetlight to count the money in his pocket – a ten pound note, a badly crumpled fiver and some loose change. He smiled and continued his brisk walk. By time he had reached the Joiner's Arms he was humming the melody from a Rachmaninov concerto.

SELF ASSEMBLY
by ADAM MAXWELL

WHERE'S the painting? The canvas, Clint – where is it?'
Big Terry pushed the gun into Clint's temple, forcing him
down to the ground, his face pressed against cardboard packaging. Clint inhaled sharply and cardboard fibres rushed into his
lungs. For once he wished for sleep. This time it didn't come.
Apparently the drugs did work. Bugger.

'I favour the Tate Modern myself,' said Big Terry, continuing an already established monologue. 'Last time I was in
London I went in there and it was inspiring. Not that I understand
all of it, mind you. And I don't think they put much thought into
people like me coming along when they hang the paintings. Well
why would they?'

'I'm not sure,' said Clint.

Big Terry stood over Clint, staring at him with little beads of
sweat starting to form above his thick, black eyebrows.

'That was a rhetorical question,' he said. 'When I want an
answer from you, it will be preceded by a sudden feeling of pain,
do you understand?'

Big Terry carefully stood on Clint's hand, he yelped and

twisted to try to extricate himself.

'Yesyesyes. Yes I understand. Jesus, this is nothing to do with me I keep telling you.'

Big Terry began walking away, looking for something.

'You can open the box now.'

Clint did as he was instructed and began to try to tear his way into whatever this flat-pack furniture Big Terry had forced him to drag out here. Of course he had been contemplating its contents ever since Big Terry turned up at his home.

It hadn't taken him long, one of his goons had kicked the door in. Clint heard Big Terry's voice then... he woke up in the boot of a car. By the time they stopped driving and opened the boot he had a very good idea what was in the box he had been lying on, however he wasn't about to admit that to himself let alone Big Terry. The cardboard quickly gave way, revealing some neatly packed pieces of wood, a plastic bag full of metal fixings and a sheet of instructions. Clint looked at them for a moment before climbing back to his feet.

'You want me to build you a desk out here?' he asked without thinking, instantly regretting it.

Big Terry stopped dead. His hand gripped the gun tighter and he turned back to face Clint, squinting in the evening sun and casting a surprisingly long shadow on the forest floor.

'Is that it?' he knew if he had made a mistake it was too late to do anything about it and instinctively went with it. 'You threaten me, you kidnap me, you drag me out here to the middle of nowhere in a blindfold, make me drag this shit all the way out here and then you want me to make you a fucking desk? Or perhaps I'm wrong, perhaps it's a nice shelving unit?'

Big Terry raised his arm and squeezed a single shot at Clint, the bullet burying itself in the tree behind him.

'I suggest you shut the fuck up and read the instructions. Now, I'm busy. I'm looking for something. I'll be around. Watching. Get building, dipshit.' He moved off into the woods out of Clint's line of sight.

Clint stared for a moment at the space Big Terry had occupied. He should make a run for it. But what was the point? Where would he go? Big Terry had picked him up at his own house, he knew about Katie and to be brutally honest he didn't really have a clue as to how to get back to wherever the hell the car was anyway. It seemed that for now furniture assembly was on the cards.

He removed the pieces of wood one by one and laid them out on the soil around him; six pieces of wood in three pairs. He knew what it was. Two of the pairs were similar, over six feet long but one pair thinner than the other. The final pair were two small squares. As he knelt down to arrange the pieces on the ground pine needles stuck sharply into his flesh.

Shelves, he thought. Perhaps Big Terry has befriended a fox in need of storage solutions.

Clint picked up the bag of fixings and tossed it from hand to hand. Carefully, he pierced the plastic with his fingers and poured out the contents onto one of the pieces of wood. He reached out a hand a spread them before finally picking up and unfolding the instructions. He looked at the list of items that should be included and stared for a second.

Two small square bits of wood. Check

Two long slim bits of wood. Check.

Two long wider bits of wood. Check.

Twenty-eight nails.

He began counting but only reached twenty-four before he ran out. Damn it. He started again, this time he had only twenty-three nails. Either way there weren't enough.

'Bi-' he began but thought better of it. Most likely Big Terry would do something unspeakable if he found out. He decided the best course of action was to do the same thing he did at home – bodge the job.

He looked back to the list and that was it. Wasn't it? He moved his index finger downwards, his lips moving as he read again.

Yes, that was it. He needed a hammer but he wasn't going to ask Big Terry for that. That was a sure fire way to get the claws lodged in the back of his head.

'You want a hammer, I'll give you a hammer,' Clint muttered under his breath, surveying the scene around him for a rock or something heavy enough to knock the nails in with. As he did so he turned over the paper in his hands to see the instructions for building the thing. His eyes widened as he stared at the page but before he could really take in what he was seeing the wind blew, catching the instructions and whipping them into the air.

'Shit!' he screamed, the air rushing from his lungs. The same voice bounced back at him from the surrounding trees after he leapt towards the instructions. Spitting guttural obscenities he hunted down the instructions, finally grabbing them once more as they caught on a small branch that he kicked at until it splintered. His tantrum over, he turned and walked calmly back towards the waiting wood, reading as he went.

The instructions were the kinds that are designed for anyone of any nationality to understand. Pictures carefully illustrated each stage of construction, four of them in total. The first picture portrayed a smiling red man standing over one of the long, wide pieces of wood that obviously served as a base for the box. He waited, hammer in hand as his smiling green friend held the two long thin pieces of wood in place.

The second picture showed the two friends nailing the end pieces in place to form a long, thin box. The red man didn't look as happy in this picture for reasons that were all too apparent.

Picture three showed the red man lying in the box while the green man nailed him in and picture four showed a section view of the red man at the bottom of a grave, nailed into his coffin and apparently banging on the lid of the casket he had just helped to build. Mr. Green stood above ground where the sun shone with a spade in one hand and a hammer in the other. Clint thought the bastard looked smug.

With a gait like a drum roll, Big Terry came scuttling out of the woods behind Clint. He spun round on the log he was perched upon but wasn't quick enough. Big Terry brought the butt of his pistol into sharp contact with Clint's temple. Clint crumpled to the ground and Big Terry stood over him, one foot either side of his head as he stared down at the blood trickling from the wound he had inflicted.

'I thought I told you not to try to escape?' he said. 'It's understandable I suppose, once you unpacked the surprise... I found what I was looking for by the way.'

'Oh good,' said Clint, trying unsuccessfully to reach up to his forehead to check his injury.

'Yes, I asked a friend of mine to come out here and dig me a big hole. Just big enough to fit that lovely box in and amazingly it is six feet deep.'

Clint raised an eyebrow; he could feel blood starting to trickle from his brow to his hairline.

'Yes, well that's why I asked him to do it isn't it?' Big Terry snapped. 'Anyway that's not the point! How did you like my instructions?'

Clint stared at Big Terry for a moment, his breathing shallow.

'Oh, this time you can speak – I really am interested to know. I designed them myself you know.'

'They blew away in the wind,' said Clint, determined not to let Big Terry know how much this really was beginning to get to him. He was pretty sure his voice only cracked once.

'I know – I saw but you read them, right?'

'Yes. I read them.'

'And?' said Big Terry, fidgeting with his gun.

'And I'm glad it's not shelving. I'm fucking hopeless at putting up shelving.'

Big Terry raised his right foot and placed it squarely on Clint's nose, exerting just the tiniest amount of pressure.

'Now Clint,' he began. 'I know you are a cocky little bastard but we can play this one of two ways. Either you can tell me what I want to know…'

Clint could smell the fresh soil between the treads on Big Terry's shoes. He tried unsuccessfully to turn his head as Big Terry began to put pressure on his face.

'Or I can and will bury you alive out here and you can starve to death in your own personal hell six feet under the ground. How does that sound?'

'Mmmmmmph,' replied Clint.

'I'll tell you what. Why don't you get going with the carpentry and you can decide in a few minutes.' Big Terry took his foot from Clint's face before kicking him in the ear.

'Ow!' Clint screamed, scrambling out of the way. 'That hurt.'

'No shit,' said Big Terry and began moving back towards the flat pack. 'Now come on, start hammering.'

A few minutes later and Clint was hammering only a few feet away from the gaping hole Big Terry had discovered.

'Terry,' said Clint.

'Big Terry.'

'Sorry, um, Big Terry. I shouldn't be here you know.'

'Oh shouldn't you? And why is that exactly?'

'I was only ever a messenger. I don't have the painting.'

'Don't play the innocent with me you little shit – you've ripped me off one too many times *boy*.'

'Wh-'

'Anyway, shut up are you nearly finished?'

Clint stood over the coffin he had constructed. The wood was rough and unvarnished.

'Listen,' said Clint. 'About that painting…'

He knew his only chance was to convince Big Terry that he really didn't know where the damn thing was but even with the pleading tone he had inadvertently adopted Big Terry remained ice cold.

'Ah yes, now we get to it.'

'I really don't know where it is,' said Clint, deflated by the response.

Big Terry stared at Clint unblinking.

'Listen, Big Terry…'

Big Terry took the pistol from his coat and cocked the hammer.

'This can't be happening, you've got to be kidding.'

He waved the pistol at Clint who shook his head.

'No, I am not getting into that fucking box.'

'Yes you are.'

Clint had begun to sweat. Not the healthy, wholesome sweat of DIY but a cold, creeping sweat that began in the small of his back and had begun working its way outwards.

'I'm really not. This… this… it's not…' Clint waved his hands in front of him and took a step back.

Big Terry got up from where he was sitting and walked across to Clint, smiling a friendly smile.

'Now Clint, earlier on I gave you a choice. I appreciate that you maintain you do not know anything about the painting. For now, I am prepared to believe you.'

'Thank God! Oh, Big Terry, I won't forget this I was really starting to panic about that whole being buried alive deal.'

Big Terry shook his head and held the barrel of his gun in front of his lips like an index finger. 'Shhhh. Earlier I gave you a choice and the choice was you either tell me where the painting is or you will be buried alive.'

Clint nodded.

'Unfortunately I don't feel I can renege on that offer and I am going to have to bury you alive.'

Clint wondered if it would make any difference if he threw up on Big Terry. He swallowed the foul gastric taste that had suddenly pervaded his palette.

'However as you didn't have the opportunity to save yourself I am going to give you a second choice.'

'Wh-?'

'I can shoot you.'

Clint stared at Big Terry as he lifted the gun and pointed it at him.

'Or not.' Big Terry raised his empty left hand and made his thumb and index finger into the shape of a gun before pulling the imaginary trigger and winking his eye.

Big Terry began to blur in front of Clint's eyes. He lifted his hand and touched his face, tears streamed down. There was nothing else he could do; he could practically feel the consciousness slipping away from him. Clint began sobbing.

'Is this dignified? Clint? Is it?' Big Terry shook his head.

'Well?'

Clint sobbed.

'I'm sorry but we really are going to have to wrap things up. I need your final answer.'

Clint shook his head.

'Okay then. In the box.'

Clint stared looked first at the box, then at the hole in the ground and, like the red man, got inside and lay down. The tears rolled down his cheeks and onto the untreated wood beneath. A splinter was sticking in his thigh but he didn't move. There was no point.

Moments later Big Terry poked his head into view. 'Actually, can you just get out for a second?'

Clint did as he was told, his eyes transfixed on the gun the whole time.

'Tall aren't you?' Big Terry grabbed the coffin and dragged it to the edge of the grave.

'I don't mean to be.'

'You can pop back in now, I just thought it'll be easier to tip you in from there.'

Clint repeated instruction number three and waited for the green man to follow through with his instructions.

Soon the lid of the coffin was in place. Big Terry, although muted, still continued talking outside.

'It's probably the best choice if I'm honest,' he said. 'If

nothing else it proves you have hope.'

With each nail that was hammered in, Clint felt the vibrations through the wood, the sound echoed in his ears and the
tears kept rolling down his face. He had stopped sobbing now
and just stared at a spot two inches in front of his face, the
claustrophobia starting to take hold.

'I mean you never know, you may be rescued.'

He had been counting the nails and he knew that there had
already been twenty-two used. That left one or two and then that
would be it.

'Not that any humans come out this far into the woods. Perhaps a passing fox will hear your cries and call his friends
together to dig you up.'

With one last bang nail number twenty-four reached its destination.

'It'll be like *Wind in the Willows*.'

Clint lay for a second trying to think of something to do, a
plan, anything. Nothing came. He could feel the coffin tilting and
after a moment it dropped, hitting the bottom of the grave,
knocking the wind out of him and winking out the light of his
consciousness. He passed out.

LIFE

by STUART WHEATMAN

THERE are very few things in life that give me pleasure these days. I can probably count on just one of my feeble little bird's claw hands the number of times I have laughed this year and we are mid-way through March!

However, this all changed when I killed my father. It has been a constant source of amusement rather than a burden of unnecessary worry, as one might have immediately assumed. Long may it continue!

It was swift and brutal – over before the unsuspecting fool worked out what was happening.

The usual morning ritual unfolded before my weary, en-crusted eyes. The sight of my father, the martyr of his own little world, waking me up for another pointless day of stale conversation and the feeling of utterly excruciating boredom filled me, as you'd expect, with unqualified gloom. This, I thought, was reason enough to plan his murder.

He dressed me in a ridiculous costume, sighing and cursing as I objected to wearing these tasteless robes. My lifeless limbs flopped around like those ineffective draft-excluding sausage-cushions that granny has dotted all over her dwelling in the home for old people they sent her to. He Heimlich-heaved me into submission. 'Asserting my authority over the human equivalent to a sack of Jersey Royals is by far a better way to start your day than Weetabix,' he undoubtedly postulated. Maintaining the continuity of this farce, I protested as only I knew how, lashing out like the uncultured pigs I'd seen drinking in the bars on the high street. Hissing and spitting was my speciality, you see, my mouth being the only usable weapon of my arsenal.

I damned him!

He was a dab hand ducking and weaving. Like every other bully you care to mention, he was a real coward; a yellow-bellied, spineless chicken; nothing more than a cockroach (although I admit to never laying eyes on one). As always, he went in for the clinch and all I could do was snarl and sink my teeth into his neck, giving him the most unexpected nip he deserved. As he recoiled, I had one last clean shot at spitting at his colossal moon face.

I'd already concluded that there wasn't a court in the land that would find me guilty of anything as ghastly as murder. I truly believe I'd be doing the world a favour worthy of eternal debt (another reason to carry out the deed). In fact, it was also my belief that the sentencing, if it could be called that, would probably unfold something like this:

'Terence Williams, we hereby find you guilty of absolutely nothing more than breathing God's fine air. To rid the world of such a crashing and tiresome bore, we would like to honour you with the key to this city, and as a gesture of goodwill, all the cake you can eat. May I also apologise for wasting your valuable time.'

Oh, what I'd give for a nice slice of cake right now. A deliciously light, fluffy strawberry sponge would be heavenly, with let's say, a generous layer of cream and a light sprinkling of icing sugar to provide the proverbial icing on the cake. Oh, my gentle companion, we mustn't digress; we simply mustn't.

Allow me to elaborate on my murderous plan once more: there I was staring at his undeniably huge globe head, with its bulging eyes and grotesque mouth screaming the most obscene of obscenities. My morning-dew spit running off its bottom lip and chin, his big gammon steak cheeks on the verge of explosion already excreting fatty sweat in an advanced state of global warming. I could almost hear the air raid sirens and people outside running to take cover in mass panic, 'Mount Williams is about to erupt. Run for your lives. Fled this disastrous village immediately!'

Quite sadly, Mount Williams' impending volcanic state was all too familiar. The bellowing and the manhandling was second nature within the confines of my home sweet home.

The outside world was very different indeed. It was a world he had little, if not no control over. We'd go about our business with my father not only supporting the girth of his huge globe head, but the weight of the world on those staunch family-man shoulders of his. His patronising tone would follow me around, banishing and impatient, menacing and mocking. Out here, I was still his prisoner. He'd manoeuvre me with no grace nor enthusiasm as though walking the Green Mile, saving the sympathetic looks for when he could reminisce about what an utterly fantastic father he is, so much kinder than that fraud Saint Nicholas and more altruistic than that Sir Bob Gandalf character. He thrived on the social stigma that I represented and was proud to be Barry Williams, Hero to the People.

Deep down, we both knew the truth. The fact that he was such a good person, kind in thought and deed, unconditionally loving, and whatever else spewed from his worn out repertoire would always be left echoing through my deaf and dumb spastic head while he left the room to punch holes in doors. I damned him again and put a curse on the miserable swine!

In my own way, I sought revenge. Whilst browsing in the most nonchalant of manners in say, a crockery section of a big department store, it wasn't unlike me to accidentally knock the odd crystal ornament over, breaking his chain of non-thought. Or scream random made up words in the strangest accents I could manage. French and Australian were clear favourites, and my Irish was just short of perfection (so it was).

My great skill was that I could invent a language at the drop of a hat, asking a passer-by the way to the station or order a ham and cheese sandwich in Skemoulevian, for example. It was during a similar linguistic expedition that I discovered, my sheer chance, my fluency in Rabocastikinion. My good chum, I shall save that episode until a more fitting tangent opportunity presents itself.

On more than one occasion in the outside world, I even pretended to have a raging fit! Imagine now the chaos and double it if you can. Similarly, this was all random – there was no set time or prepared performance nor was there any rehearsal – it was all improvised to generate maximum embarrassment for my tormentor: the lingerie department of Marks and Spencer, a crowded fast food restaurant or an art gallery were all worthy venues. It took little to no thought in order to get into character. I simply played on the universal perception of society, when ogling a specimen such as myself.

My modus operandi was and is as follows: connect with everyone who displays pitiful looks. Engage eye contact with those who look away in disgust. Use a somewhat manic and unstable expression. This can be practiced in advance, but is easily achieved by tilting one's head to the side at a thirty-degree angle and rolling one's eyes to the top of one's head, fluttering the eyelids. Spasms must ensue in order to instil fear into the unsuspecting public. Jerking one's head back, lurching and hunching like a moronic demon; an absent, open mouth and loose tongue confirming their suspicions that you are indeed a living, breathing vegetable. Konstantin Stanislavski is a name I am unfamiliar with, and yet I have perfected the method of which he taught.

Spitting is the key, dribbling – the stringier the better and some mucus can never hurt either. If you can cling onto someone and deliver an outburst of ghoulish moaning, nay, banshee wailing, then you are truly a refined expert in the field of fits.

Children and young women are the likeliest of victims – their reaction is always by far the most hysterical. The beauty of this trick is that the commendation usually directed toward my dear father quickly turns ugly. He is frequently labelled a hate figure on our outings, thanks to me; 'Look at that bastard dragging that poor kid around in that state,' said one old dear to her dear old dear friend. Indeed, if I hadn't decided to kill him, he'd be as popular as the vilest of sexually transmitted diseases.

Caught in this predicament, more often than never at all he reverts back to cursing and obscenities. He does this as though I, his disfigured genetic nightmare of a failed son, orchestrated such a scene of utter distress.

'It's all down to bad parenting,' they mutter. 'What kind of a man would inflict such a terrible ordeal as shopping on such a decrepit creature?'

Then it's me who gets their vote in the Sympathy Elections. I sob, begging for mercy, calling out for help from a Samaritan in the crowd of onlookers as I'm wheeled out.

Doing such stunts was my main pleasure, as I say, before I decided to kill him. I toyed with the idea for 27 hours before planning it in detail. I may be inexperienced in the act of murder, but I'm not completely naïve. Far from it. I knew there was no call for an over-elaborate plan, no matter how cunning. All that was required was a simple idea. Indeed that simple idea came to me, well, quite simply. There would be no poisons, guns, knives or ropes. All I needed to do was crush his head. His huge globe head. I'd crush it, to coin a phrase, like a grape.

I decided to initiate this plan on Saturday morning. He got me dressed and ready for the swimming baths in his customary manner, abruptly pulling me this way and that, combing my hair into a ridiculous Hitler-parting and feeding me some mashed up excuse for food that would cause even a stray dog to vomit.

I kept my cool; I complied. He was noticeably surprised at the lack of drama, but there was another surprise to come.

My dear mother was already in the car waiting as my father strapped me into my special seat. As he made the final adjustments, I realised the opportunity and grabbed it. Taking my right hand up to my eye and using my thumb and forefinger as my sight, I focused, closing my left eye, squinting, tracking him like a sniper until I had a clear shot.

I could see the uncertainty in his tiny mind. He turned briefly to attract my mother's attention, and then I let him have it. I crushed his head in one go; my thumb and forefinger like a powerful Ostrich beak, snapping together like pincers.

It was never my intention to kill him in front of his own wife, but needs must.

As I released the pincers, he was there, still in my eye line, gawping and stuttering. I couldn't resist crushing his stupid head once more. C-rrrusssshhhh.

He still had the same gammon-esque cheeks and the annoyingly huge head, but now his big sweaty face wore a smile and he directed what appeared to be words of encouragement toward my very being.

Mother had turned round in her seat to witness the miracle. Like a performing seal, I crushed my father's head again to rapturous applause. Encore, *encore!*

I was given a white chocolate mouse to suck on; which could only be a consolation prize in comparison to my newly acquired knowledge. It seemed to me that murder was not quite the crime I first thought it to be. Though I will tell you this, it took great effort not only to squeeze the retched man's head, but to successfully create and use the dormant tools of my murderous trade. I was also suitably impressed.

It was whilst thrashing around in the shallow end of the little pool, eyes streaming with chlorine, clinging on for dear life to the man whose head I'd just crushed; that my mind again began to wander.

There was my mother, my dear mother, sitting in the balcony with her enormous right-angled dice of a head buried into some soulless novel as though she hadn't a care in the world. A distinct lack of worry lines across Frankenstein's Monstress head told only of her lack of concern for your dear narrator, not her youthfulness. Likewise of a flowing mane, showing no signs of natural highlights, as opposed to the wispy dome that father sometimes referred to as hair. She looked up on occasion to force a weak preoccupied smile, quickly returning to her thirty-something dinner-party world of escapism. How dare she! I damned her immediately!

All this time I'd been at war with my beloved father, when all along we should have been on the same side. Was he not just as downtrodden as I? Was he just as trapped and worthless? I double-damned the scheming witch. She had some nerve, of that I am certain.

If there was one good gene I'd inherited from her, it was her audacity. No apparent consequence to crushing my father's head would surely mean I could also get away with crushing that unsightly shoebox-looking monstrosity. I concocted my new plan as my father dried me and dressed me. He heaved me around to the point of exhaustion, yet I never once had the urge to end his life. Nevertheless, my slack-jawed dribble quite deliberately landed on his (now crushed) head as he tied my shoelaces. You cannot expect anything but uncouth from a calculated killer as I, would be my disclaimer.

As we set off to drive us the 3.2 miles back home, I knew that by the time we reached our destination I'd have disposed with my dear mother. I'd wait until we hit the motorway, then I'd crush that outrageously cubic hideousness of hers without a second thought.

FLUX

by DAVID WATSON

THE phone calls triggered me. Eventually.

I never took much notice for the first few months. Just wrong numbers. Mixed in with auto-dial sales calls from the subcontinent. The latter always came when I was at the farthest or most inconvenient point in the house or at the bottom of the garden. I didn't get that many calls on the landline so never felt the need to carry the phone with me. Having been divorced for a year or so it was good to get a call – so I'd break my neck to get to the phone before the caller gave up or left a message.

– Hello.

My greeting was always followed by the ominous silence of a computer thousands of miles away piping my voice into an operator's ears and my profile onto their screen.

– Am I speaking to Mr Vincent?

I always put the phone down at that point.

Disappointment gave way to frustration, which in turn gave way to anger, which eventually resolved itself through a call to the sales call blocking service I saw advertised on TV. They sent me a letter to confirm my registration. They couldn't telephone, obviously. Unfortunately the letter informed me they couldn't block unsolicited calls originating from outside of the UK. Great, my accented friends would still be calling me at inopportune moments then. My disgruntlement was tempered as the calls dried up over the next couple of weeks. The callers' origins were obviously no further south than Dover. My mistake. At last something promised to me had been fulfilled. Pity I hadn't had the call monitoring service look after my divorce.

So it was amongst this newfound serenity that I began noticing the wrong numbers. After a while I connected them to the letters that weren't for me either – but not at first.

I had been in the house around six months. Settled in well. Met all the neighbours. Decided which ones were to be avoided, which ones to be acknowledged, which ones to be engaged. This took a while. My new home was in a cul-de-sac but the number of neighbours seemed exponential to the number of homes. My greetings were frequently mumbled as someone bid me good morning or good evening as I jumped in or out of my car and they from theirs. They all seemed to recognise me but then there was only one of me. There seemed to be dozens of them. Obviously. I resolved to send them all a Christmas card from 'Pete at No 23' in order to put names to faces, faces to doors and cars, and so improve my recall and cul-de-sac-cred. I could do the exponential stuff a bit myself when I put my mind to it.

My new house gradually became a home as rooms were filled, in a minimalist way. The neutral paint scheme I had purchased with the house gave way to swathes of colour on some feature walls and I bagged some decent furniture in a never-ending sale. I even created the right space for the home cinema I once owned. In that space squatted a 14-inch portable – the one remnant of a previous life. I didn't have the remote.

Sometimes, when I was away for a few days, there would be a pile of envelopes waiting on my doormat, at other times there would be none. Credit card companies spent a small fortune on promotional material to entice me. As did charities. Both might as well have been writing direct to the Italian designed stainless steel waste bin I had bought on impulse to throw my solicitor's letters in, because that's where their communications went, unopened usually, sometimes torn in half if I was feeling particularly lonely. Over time there seemed to be an increasing number of people writing to my house but not to me.

The letters were a mild inconvenience. To start with. There was a post box not far away and I'd neatly add 'Not at this address' to the misplaced letters and re-post them. After a couple of months I realised this was having no effect as the letters kept coming. I reasoned that unless there was a return address then I was simply adding to the confusion. This was a watershed in my communications difficulties. From this point onwards to save the post office and my own small inconvenience, the Italian pedal bin was fed any misplaced letters as an aperitif to the bulky credit card applications and cheap-pen-containing charity letters. I assumed that the people writing would eventually give up once they received no reply from my home address. The writers were tenacious though, even if ill-advised as to the whereabouts of their friends and relatives. Come to think of it so were the charity organisations. I began to realise they were not just sending their paper begging bowls to me at my house but to other people at the same address. And I most definitely lived alone. In fact the only people who had their data-addressing shit together were the credit card companies and my ex-wife's solicitor.

The BBC wrote frequently too. Or rather their licensing dogs did. They seemed to be a little confused about me. They knew I lived at 23 Westmorland Park. They knew I had a TV. But they were in dispute with themselves about whether or not I had a license. I did have one – I had the paper copy and a direct debit to prove it. This didn't stop them writing to me threatening a hefty fine and/or imprisonment. Our dialogue was ongoing – like my own personal soap opera.

Like the Beeb, the utility companies seemed to be somewhat

lax in their operations too. I grew increasingly frustrated – not with the quality or standard of their product, but with the amount of fucking meter reading cards I found shoved through my door. Each time I dutifully read the meters – gas, water, electric – filled the cards in and then relayed the information back. Firstly, I tried leaving the card outside the door for the meter man who indicated I should do so. Next time, I dialled the meter line and left my readings on an answerphone. Then I tried email – blipping the digits to some made up name somewhere in a meter reading conglomerate. Finally, I even logged on to the bastard's website, punched the digits into a drop down box, pressed send and received a nice little thank you from the server. Two days later – another fucking green card on my mat. Bin.

I was getting attuned to the waste pouring through my letter-box from corporate world but after a while I began spotting misplaced personal correspondence on a regular basis.

And then yesterday, having been away on business for a particularly lonely week, I returned to just one letter staring up at me from the hall mat. I recognised the name – not mine – but I still recognised it. Mrs C Vincent. I put down my case, locked the door behind me and walked through to the kitchen, letter in hand. I pressed the pedal at the base of the silver bullet of a bin. The gas-damped lid eased itself back with a predatory gape. It was then I decided to open the letter. I removed my foot and the mouth clamped shut.

Hi Christine. Sorry you didn't get my last letter. Don't know what happened there but at least we got to talk on the phone briefly, which was nice. Thought I'd write to you anyway just to prove I can still do longhand and not just txt ;)

And so it went on. Deeply uninteresting, but nevertheless unsettling. Unsettling because surely the writer checked she had the correct address of Mrs C Vincent when she spoke to her on the phone and surely *Christine* told *Angie* that she had the wrong bloody address. Obviously not. I checked the envelope again. *Christine's* name. *My* address. I fed envelope and letter to the gas damped mouth.

So last night I drank ink-black cinnamon tequila, topped up with Coke, chilled with ice. As the evening spiralled slowly towards a full night sprawled on the sofa, my flagging eyes settled on the phone in its rather dusty cradle. I resolved to clean the thing the next morning as I lifted it to check for messages. I pressed a green symbol and the phone beeped irregularly to tell me someone had called. I dialled the auto message box.

– *You have, two, new messages. Message, one, left, Monday, October, twenty-fourth, at, six, fifteen, pm.*

– Pete it's me. I'm assuming you're away. When you get back can you please respond to the letter. It is important. Bye.

– *Message, two, left, today, at five, eighteen, pm.*

– Hi Christine, it's Angie. I'm up in town tomorrow and was going to call in for a coffee if you're going to be in babe. Probably be about ten in the morning. Give me a call and let me know – if I don't hear from you I'll just take a chance and call anyway. Hope you got my letter this time. Gottago. See you tomorrow hopefully. Bye.

I hadn't received the first letter intended for me and had binned the second one. I couldn't communicate with the woman I needed to, and now had another woman about to visit me because she thought someone else lived in my house. Great. I fiddled about with the phone to try and get a dial back on the number to put an end to the confusion. I managed to delete both messages and get a symbol I hadn't seen before on the screen of the phone. I dropped the phone back in its cradle and took another swig from my glass.

I got to thinking about the following morning and whether I should delay my journey to work in order to wait for Angie's visit. Or I could leave a note on the door. Or I could just ignore the problem – it wasn't of my making after all. But then the calls and the letters would continue to find me. I slipped off the sofa and crawled across the floor to change the channel. I would decide in the morning. I crawled back to my warm space on the sofa like a beaten cur and squinted at the TV. Football was not designed for transmission on portable televisions.

The sunlight found me face down on the sofa this morning. I'd forgot to close the curtains. Forgot to go to bed. It seemed early. I couldn't check my watch immediately because I'd fallen asleep with my left arm tucked underneath my head. To all purposes the limb was dead for the minute. I heaved myself over and my shoulder pulled the errant arm upwards. It moved like a sleeve full of wet sand. Once on my side, the circulation began to seep back and my fingertips twitched erratically. The arm felt even heavier and I shook it spastically, clenching and unclenching my fist. I checked my watch. It was 8:23 and I knew that by the time I pulled myself together I would be sitting in traffic for an hour. I resolved to wait until 10:00 instead. Kill two birds with one stone.

I ate a single slice of toast and drank black coffee and an orange juice. The injection of food and liquid stimulated me and made me hungry. I showered, dressed and then gave in to the hunger and ate a bowl of cereal. It was 9:05 and a misplaced guilt began to get the better of me. For some reason I felt like I was defrauding someone of work time. I wasn't. I'd spent at least sixty to seventy hours of the last three weeks grinding out the hours. The last thing I owed anyone was an hour of my time. I pulled some files to work on from my brief case, but found my mind drifting from what I was looking at to what I was thinking of.

Was I getting paranoid about these misplaced identities that seemed to be seeking out a home where I had chosen to live? Since separating from my wife I had felt a sense of loss – not of her or our relationship but of self. We had not been together forever – seven or so years – but that passage of time obviously shapes both people. Once that pattern had been removed there was, inevitably perhaps, a move to a condition of flux for me – at least for a while until I found a new shape. Once I had my house though I'd felt stronger, more in control. A sense of stability had returned – the bills, the mortgage, the repairs, the chores – all these controlling elements and others built a platform that I had to operate on. Strange how such restrictions scaffolded my fragile life at that point but they did. And as I'd grown secure in my new independence my bruised confidence regained something like its true colour and I was feeling more able to get on with living. But…

…but now these crossed wires troubled me. They were nothing and something at the same time.

Just last week I had returned home from work to find a car parked across my drive. It wasn't a model I recognised as belonging to one of the neighbours. I lived in a narrow cul-de-sac and there was only room to park on one side of the street, or on a drive if the homeowner had one. The fact that most houses had more than one car made parking an issue at times. I had waited patiently for a minute or so and then gave a short blast on the horn. No response. One more, longer. Still nothing. I couldn't get on the drive and couldn't park nearby as the cars were nose to tail the length of the road. I executed a seven-point turn at the head of the cul-de-sac and revved down the road again. I pulled round the corner, parked and fumed back up to my house on foot.

Twenty minutes later, as I waited hawk-like at the front window, a woman came down from a house two or three doors up and approached the offending car.

– Excuse me, I said.

She looked up.

– Any chance of you not parking across my drive next time you visit?

– Sorry – Ronnie said there was no one living here. She gestured up the street to the house she had emerged from.

– I've been living here six months.

– Well I didn't know. Sorry. I've never seen your car either so when Ronnie said park here I didn't think it would be a problem.

– Right. Well you know now so can I take it I'll be able to

get on my drive next time you visit Ronnie?

– Yes. I've said sorry haven't I? No one died did they? Okay?

She dismissed me. Got in the car. Turned the engine over. Crunched it into reverse. Jerked the car backwards. Then hopped it forwards and sped off down the street.

She was right. It was no big deal. But the fact that the man up the street hadn't realised someone had been living in my house for six months had somehow aggrieved me. Was I so invisible? So indistinctive? Unnoticeable?

So while I thumbed through a bunch of papers, waiting to chastise another innocent, the creeping anxiety returned. In my head I thumbed through the wrong letters, the wrong numbers, the misinformed neighbours and joined them all together in the hope of creating an answer. A single reason. Something beyond pure coincidence. I failed.

I checked my watch – it was 9:55. What was I going to say to this woman then? Something simple. Straightforward. You are mistaken. You have the wrong address. The wrong telephone number. Your friend does not live here.

I waited until 10:15 but no one arrived. That could mean a variety of things. I didn't bother to begin thinking what. There was a sense of relief that I did not want to waste. I grabbed my coat and briefcase, armed the house alarm, locked the front door, disarmed the car alarm, opened the door and jumped in. I slotted the card and pressed the starter button. The engine fired into life. I turned down the volume on the CD, selected drive and eased off the mock-cobbles.

At the bottom of the cul-de-sac I waited for a gap in the stream of traffic still snaking its way into the city centre. I needed to cut across it to head the other way. I tapped at the wheel while I waited for someone to let me out. A red Toyota flashed me and I pushed my nose out across the nearside lane. I gestured my thanks and then turned my attention to traffic coming the other way. Cars streamed by and then one slowed to a stop just to my left. I hesitated then realised the car was indicating to turn in to my street. I looked up at the driver and she flashed me a smile and pointed ahead of her. I was like a rabbit. The red Toyota driver grew impatient and gave me a gentle prod with a flash of his lights. I over-revved and rode the clutch as my car eased out in front of the turning car. I tried to smile my acknowledgement to the woman but the angles were all wrong by then. I straightened up and glanced in my rear mirror. She was still waiting to turn as the Toyota driver's politeness evaporated. I raised my hand to signal my thanks and I think she smiled again. Angie.

Today at work I wasn't able to get her face in or out of my head. I couldn't remember her because I didn't quite see her this morning. I couldn't forget her because I was so sure she was going to call at my house to visit her friend Christine. So sure. Why else would she be turning into a cul-de-sac? I was sure she wasn't a neighbour. My day was wasted wondering about this non-event not taking place at my house.

Tonight as I drove home from work I resolved to put this crap behind me and get on with life without worrying about such inconsequential shit. I determined that I had ended up focussing on this stuff over the last few weeks as an intentional form of self-deception. Like a magician I was using misdirection to prevent a focus on the things that were really important. However, most magicians misdirected their audience, not themselves. I needed to move on, not slip back into the malaise that I had found myself wading through a few months earlier. Recognising this fact had broken the spell. I drove too fast for the last three miles of my journey

By the time I pulled onto my drive this evening I was buzzing. The endorphins were coursing through me as I sensed a sea change in my attitude. I breezed into the house, setting off the alarm as I failed to punch the digits in correctly. Having quelled the noise I scooped up the envelopes from the floor. Walking through the hall to the kitchen I sorted them. Two out of four for me. Glass half-full then. The other two I did not register apart from the fact they weren't for me and in the bin they went with a satisfying gas-damped metallic clamp. I decided to go for a run so chugged some juice from a carton in the fridge and swallowed four slightly stale jaffa cakes with barely a chew between them. I changed quickly into some running gear, removed the door key from its bunch and headed out, locking the door behind me. I ran for exactly 45 minutes and 17 seconds and covered around 6 miles, which was good. While I ran I thought about nothing of any consequence. I did think about a new car for a brief period as a shiny BMW whistled past me at one point, but apart from that I was in the zone – that place where you just put one foot in front of the other and check your watch when it feels like you've done a mile. It was fantastic. The way everything in life should be. I got back. Stretched. Finished the juice from the carton. Cooled down. Resolved to buy a new television at the weekend. Jumped in the shower. Thought about the HDTV option. Dried off. Put on some jeans and a t-shirt. Thought about dinner. Decided on a take-away. Flicked on the portable. Selected the least offensive programme. Sat back on the sofa and stretched out my arms. My left arm brushed against the telephone, almost knocking it from its cradle. I put it back and then picked it up. I pressed the green button. An undulating, cyclical beeping told me I had a message. I should have ignored it, but couldn't. As I pressed the digits of the retrieve code I felt one kind of easy energy ebb from me to be replaced with a tension that strung me like a catapult.

That was twenty minutes ago. Since then I've been review-ing the day; reviewing the last few weeks; last few months. Been listening to the two new messages on my answerphone. I'm trying to piece things together because something's not right. Definitely not right.

I'm going to play the first message again now:

– Hi Christine. It's Angie. I know you've only just got rid of me – well a few hours ago. But I've just found out Charlotte's pregnant. How much were we not expecting that then! Anyway if you're coming up next week, we'll call and see her. Glad you're settling in to the new place and I do love what you're doing with the big colours and snappy furniture. That little TV has got to go though. For sure. Great seeing you. Keep it together babe. We'll have a blast next week. See ya.

It was her. In the car. Earlier today. I'm sure. Positive. She's been here. In my house. But someone else was here. Christine was here. Is she here now? Am I here now? This is screwing me up. Something's tipped upside down. Things are falling out. Listen to this next message and tell me things aren't sliding:

– Hello. Christine? Christine pick up. Okay I guess you're out or not in the mood to talk. Look I'm sorry, okay. I got it wrong. I shouldn't have said what I did. It just seemed a little odd what you were telling me but I'm prepared to talk about it now. If you do see Angie tell her I'm sorry about the letters. I shouldn't have done that either. She's only trying to help. I know. I'd like to come home Christine. I really miss you. I know I've been acting strange and stuff, but I've got my head round it now and I think we can make it work. I'll call tonight again – around 8:30. Please be there when I call Christine. Please.

I recognise the voice straightaway.

It's me. No doubt about it.

I didn't make that call though. The timecode says it was left at 7:30 tonight. I was still running then. But it's me. No doubt.

Things are definitely sliding. Sliding away.

My watch says 8:27. Three minutes.

This is my home. I'm sure.

My address. Of that I am certain.

My neighbours. Though they don't seem to know me.

It's just turned 8:28.

That's my shitty little TV in the corner too.

My bold paint on that feature wall.

And my snappy furniture – a piece of which I'm sitting on right now.

Not Christine's. Whoever she is.

8:29 now.

By my watch.

8:30.

And this is my phone ringing.

I'm going to take it. Take the call. I have to take the call.

– Hello

– Am I speaking to Mr Vincent?

GOD

by LUKE WATSON

WHENEVER there's an emergency happening, an accident, incident, some tragedy, and people are dying or are holed up in hospital for an extended length of time, my associates give me the call to go out and look for surviving orphans. The kids usually appreciate someone to talk to. I swan in, dressed elegant in my white robe, and I let the kids touch my hair shirt – kids love to rub the hair shirt – and then I ask them where their parents have got to. Three times out of four the answer is satisfactory and I whisk them from the waiting room, the bar, the hotel, or on occasions you see them on the beach, and introduce them to Mr. Isles, or Deirdre, his German receptionist with the goofy teeth and the pet Chihuahua named Sanchez.

One of the first kids I ever picked up was Cuthbert, a nine year old with streaky blonde hair and a fascination with goldfish and death. Kids can be beautiful, I've always said. They have this aura, this fleeting disregard that makes them kids, and who am I to say what people can and cannot find attractive? Cuthbert was beautiful. The time I found her, after a hotel fire, she had on khaki pants and a t-shirt that said *Jesus Died For You, But He's*

Coming Back For Me.

Best of all, though, the thing I remember most was someone had given her a light blue dressing gown and she was spinning around in it with the ends flying up, catching the wind. She looked distinctive. I can always see the distinctive ones, which is why they pay the big money for my services. A nurse was telling her to occupy herself while the doctors saw to her parents.

I sat down in front of the girl. The Cuthbert couple were not going to make it, I could see it in the way the nurse had touched the child. The girl stopped spinning and looked straight at me, hoping to recognise my face. I smiled. She asked me my name and I told her my name was God. She shook her head and said there is only one God.

'Are you God?' she asked, 'Can you help my mom and dad?'

I told her I would try, but I wasn't God.

'My name's Godric,' I said.

'Is that a real name?' she asked.

By the time her parents were pronounced dead, we were gone to get something to eat. I knew a waitress at a restaurant nearby called Melinda. She always said I would make a wonderful father. I introduced Cuthbert as another of my nieces.

'What a beauty,' Melinda said.

She and Cuthbert shook hands and I ordered myself a drink. Cuthbert sat on a chair with her spiked orange juice. She kept pulling at my jacket saying we should be getting back to the hospital. Melinda would have been easy, but I needed to get Cuthbert off the island. She was already drowsy and in my arms when I skipped out on the bill, followed down the street by Melinda calling out the fake name I had given her.

Me and Cuthbert stayed as the best of friends as our situation allowed for the next couple of months, after that I said goodbye and she looked at me bruised and defeated and cried that I was heartless. I think I probably nodded and said that all this was just what I did. There was going to be a civil war somewhere down in

South America. I had seen the street fighting and the bloody riots in a dream. There would be plenty of easy business if I got to the capital before the uprising started. Anyway, I had to leave eventually. Cuthbert knew that from the beginning. I left her in good hands. Santiago ran some clean businesses and a few dirty ones. I knew Santiago to be a good man, never foolish with his money or his children. He took a shine to Cuthbert like everyone did at first. I was out of Italy a week later and went back to Louisiana for some fishing, some drinking and the women. I was never home for long. I had this cabin on the water front, which was pretty as hell and took my mind off my work. That was all back going on ten years now. A hundred or so kids have entered my life and left it just as quick since then. I hardly think of each one as different from the other.

I wake up and check my messages. A call from mama, one from Alec about a little easy money in Texas, and another from someone speaking incoherently in Spanish about Jesus. They leave a number so I dial it. Someone picks up and all I hear is screaming.

'Que?' a woman says.

'It's God, I'm returning a message. Who is this?' I yell back.

'I get Compo,' she says and puts the phone down. I wait for Compo.

'Godric?' he says, as the screaming dies down.

'Yeah, it's me. What's happening there?' I ask.

'There's some work. I told them you would go,' Compo says. 'We have a nice deal at a hospital in Jerusalem, needs organising and carrying out.'

I shake my head. 'Compo, don't agree my work for me. I find my own work,' I tell him.

'Look, you go? We have many people there. Yes?'

I do not need to think it over. I say yes.

A driver greets me at the airport.

'God?' he asks. 'May I?'

I hand him my bag, but he shakes his head. He wants to touch my hair shirt. I get into the car and he jumps into the front. He asks me about my flight and about work at the hospital. He acts like a kid. He looks a lot like a child too, but he drives the car like an old man, slow and dangerously. I ask him who he works for.

'Mr. Isles,' the driver says, smiling at me in the rear-view mirror.

'He's here?' I ask. 'What about Santiago?'

The driver nods. 'But I have orders to take you straight to the hospital. You have your fun tonight, yes. Work now.'

I nod. 'Sure,' I say, 'Work now.'

The driver stops the car on a back street. Everywhere around us is peaceful and pretty, except for the in and out goings of the hospital on the other side of the road. The kid opens my door and I climb out.

'We cross over to the other side,' he says and winks, grinning. I nod and smile to him. He pats me on the back with his empty hand and we walk around the hospital.

'Julio,' a voice says.

The kid stops and turns into an open door. We follow a female nurse down a busy and well-lit corridor until we reach an office. The nurse kisses Julio on the cheek and then leaves us. He watches her strut away and then raises an eyebrow at me.

'I like them a little older than, well,' he pauses and then shakes his head. We wait outside the door, it never occurring to the kid that he might have to knock.

The door opens and Deirdre almost stumbles over when she sees me.

'He said it was a big job, but he never said it was a job for God,' she laughs in her ugly, neutral accent. 'Come, come. Sit down, I fetch Martin.'

She walks through the room and into another. Julio hugs me.

'Here I will say my goodbyes,' he says. 'But I will drive you to hotel, yes?'

I nod yes and he lets go of me, dropping from tiptoes onto the soles of his fake leather shoes. He slaps his hands together and closes the door behind him. Deirdre shuffles back in and beckons that I follow her with her worn out and gold-ringed index finger.

Mr. Isles is a fine Englishman. As soon as I walk into his little office I know it can only be him. His desk is hidden by high piles of paper and medical files. He has a row of pills lined up in front of him. He blows cigar smoke into an electric fan.

'Here he is,' Deirdre cries either to me or to him and either about me or about him. Mr. Isles stands up and shakes my hand. He nods for his assistant to leave, and she makes her own way out, but a large and leathery muscle man remains seated on a cardboard box in the corner of the room.

'How was your trip?' Mr. Isles asks.

'Sudden,' I tell him.

He sits back, relaxed and ready for business.

'I guess you know why you're here. It's a nice set-up, but it's the usual one. You know how it is.'

I look him straight in the eye, which is my way of showing I understand.

'Good. That's the reason I hire you, Godric, I don't need to waste my time explaining myself. I sent that damn Scot to Texas, I have to explain everything. You know Alec?' he asks.

I nod. 'He talks about you and your hair shirt. Says if he had the hair shirt he'd be getting ten kids a day. Ten.'

He laughs and I keep staring straight at him.

'Kids love the hair shirt,' I say.

Mr. Isles nods his head, 'That brute is crazy. He's hopeless at his job, hair shirt or without. You know what I have him doing now?'

I shrug.

'I have him beating the life out of traitors, and sometimes the men who don't pay.' He laughs, 'But mainly traitors.'

He leans forward and stares at me. I remain still. Sometimes

Mr. Isles likes to stare at people. We sit in silence and then he smiles happily.

'You start tomorrow, it's late tonight.'

I stand up and so does he. The big guy in the corner struggles to his feet as well.

'That's Avner,' Mr. Isles laughs hysterically. 'Look at him,' he says. 'He's wearing a sports jacket.'

I smile and make my way back outside to the car. All the way I can hear Mr. Isles laughing.

Julio opens the door for me and I get in thanking him.

'So, sir, where are we going now?'

He starts the engine and pulls out into the road. He looks up into the rear-view mirror, his eyes flicking back and forth, on me and on the street ahead.

'Do you know where Santiago can be found?'

Julio nods, 'Oh yes,' he grins. 'I can always find Mr. Santiago.'

He raises an eyebrow in my direction. 'You have your fun now, eh?' he says.

'Yeah,' I say, 'Fun now.'

The terraced buildings in a line up and down to the right and left of us look dormant and plainly residential. Santiago must have fallen hard to go from villas in Spain and apartments in Rome to here. There was a time when people respected his kindness and business strategy. Now he's running drugs and prostitute rings down back alleys in Jewish holy land. Julio knocks at the door. The curtain of the window draws back and the dark eyes of a man appear and examine Julio's happy face. The man says something, maybe in Hebrew, and Julio responds. The door opens and we step in.

The main room has fallen quiet and is brightly lit by tall candles. The doorman slaps me on the back and whistles up the stairs. A woman calls the name of Santiago. I stand with my back to the wall as a seven year old girl tours my legs, clapping and looking at me in a stage of distraught tranquillity. Santiago enters the room, throws his arms wide open and picks the girl up.

'My good friend,' he says to me, kissing my cheeks and running a hand through my hair.

He passes the girl to a middle-aged woman with an eye patch and discoloured skin.

'My daughter and my wife,' Santiago shrugs and gestures for me to sit down. He studies me carefully, laughing and lighting a cigarette.

'You look well,' he says. 'How do you feel? Well?'

As he speaks he moves his hand, dancing the orange burn of the cigarette across the room, leaving a strange, rising pattern of smoke.

'I'm doing fine,' I say after a moment of thought.

'What are you doing in my part of the world?' he asks.

I tell him about the hospital and my latest visions of worldwide tragedy.

'It's impending then, this apocalypse?' he laughs.

I shrug and look over at Julio. He talks to the lady with the eye patch and plays a game of hide and seek with the child. For a while we sit in silence, enjoying the mood and the heavy air.

'You must be wanting a drink,' Santiago says, cursing his bad manners. I shake my head.

'No. Look, I can't stay long. I have a favour to beg.'

He looks around the room. 'You turn down my offer of a drink?' he asks.

'I cannot stay, Santiago.'

He takes my hand in his. 'You will be back. This will become your new home,' he says and blinks slowly.

'The favour,' I repeat.

'Yes, of course.'

I tell him about Cuthbert. I remind him of his part in her life. I tell him I am looking for her. I tell him I want him to help me find her. He sits back in his stained armchair and takes the cigarette from his mouth.

'What was her name again? Her full name?'

I shrug with unknowing and he sighs. 'You must remember,' I say. 'Everybody loved her.'

Santiago stares at my face with a blank look on his own. He shrugs and laughs,

'I can find this girl, Godric. I will find out what happened to this Cuthbert girl.'

I nod and get up to leave. 'How long will it take?' I ask.

He kisses my cheeks once more and leads me to the door.

'It will be soon, I assure you. This is the least I owe.'

Julio grins and pats a seven year old orphan on the back of the head. I try to make out the emotion in the boy's eyes. I take it to be abject confusion. I tell him not to worry and ask him if he can speak Danish.

He shakes his head. I smile and say, 'You'll learn,' as Julio leads him away through the cardboard boxes and stacks of paper that decorate Mr. Isles' office.

Three Jewish bodyguards play a murder mystery board game in the corner of the room, although they occasionally run around shooting at each other with their index fingers out-stretched. Deirdre coughs as usual, spluttering and choking, before spitting blood onto the floor and smearing the stain with the sole of her shoe until it has faded and disappeared. She puts her hands on her knees, her body bent double and her wide mouth gasping for oxygen. I walk into my office and chalk off another boy as Sold and Delivered.

The telephone rings and I pick it up. There are photographs and drawings on my desk. I spread them out before me as I wait for the operator to connect us through the complicated hospital telephone system. I keep the pencil drawings on one side and the pictures of the kids on the other. I play the game of matching up what is wanted with what is available here. The telephone clicks.

'Godric,' a heavy voice murmurs.

'Who is this?' I ask.

'Godric, it's Santiago. I have news about the girl you were looking for. *The girl.*'

I sit down and leave the pictures for later.

'Santiago, what have you found?'

He breathes out and says nothing. I wait, tapping my foot against a table leg.

'I traced her back,' Santiago says. 'I traced her all the way back. Where you got her, where I sent her, I have it all here. I tracked her down. I have found her.' He sounds excited and pleased with himself.

'So?' I ask.

'Can you come to the house?' he says.

'Why can't you tell me now?'

He hums and says, 'Cannot you see I am on the telephone?'

I keep listening, waiting for him to return. 'Godric?' he asks. 'Yeah?'

'Please, will you just come to the house?'

I finish work organising a meeting between Mr. Isles and an Egyptian with a taste for girls rolled up in rugs. Julio drives me to Santiago's home smoking a cigarette and mumbling to himself about the city's broken future. I watch outside pass in bright lights and wandering businessmen from the safety of the car. Julio stops and nods for me to get out. He drives off without saying a word, something hanging heavy over his usually bright demeanour.

I knock three times on Santiago's door and it swings open.

'Godric, that you?' a voice calls from inside.

I enter and flick on a light switch.

'It's me,' I say and close the door behind me.

'Come in and sit down. I be out in a moment,' the voice calls back.

I take my place in my favourite chair and pick up a magazine filled with pencil drawings of children doing what some people think children should be doing while they're still young. It's an American publication, the short stories of adult fantasies and articles proving the theory of false memory as fact are printed in stylised English.

Santiago walks in with a folder in one hand and a drink in the other.

'Put that down, Godric and look at this,' he says, sitting opposite me.

I throw the magazine to the floor and take the folder from him.

'I found the girl. Her name is Abigail. Her real name is Abigail.'

He smiles at me as I look through his information, the photographs, the forms and business transactions, a score of her physical beauty, marked out of ten, it's all here.

'Thank you, Santiago,' I say.

He nods and takes a drink. 'Would you like anything?' he asks.

I left Cuthbert in Rome where she stayed for three years. Once Santiago passed her on the details in the forms become a little confused. She probably lived and worked for the next five years in a small Dutch town on the German border, but that could be far from the truth.

'Where is she now?' I ask.

Santiago turns over a few pages and points at an official looking contract. 'England,' he says.

I read over the words, touching them with the tips of my fingers.

'Durham, England,' I read out loud. 'Where's Durham?'

Santiago shrugs, 'It's in England.'

I find Finchale a week later with a rented car, a map holed with cigarette burns and a recommendation from Mr. Isles to go fishing in the river Wear. He smacked his lips when he said it, repeating the words *prime salmon*. I nodded and left the hospital having done the job I was brought over to do. I was finished with the work now anyway. Mr. Isles just sat open-mouthed when I told him I was done with the business, when I told him I was sick of myself and sick of him. I told him he was going to hell, but I was going to save myself. Then I turned and walked out as quickly as I had stormed in. He never said a word in return. I wrapped my hands around Deirdre's head and told her to kill herself. I gave Julio everything I wasn't taking with me and paid Santiago double for his troubles. When I had cut off all ties with the men I used to call friends I left, quietly slipping away on the first flight back to my homeland, without a thank you or a goodbye to tide me over.

I wade out into the cold waters of the river. In the distance the beauty of the abbey removes every evil thought and fills me with the desire to do right by Cuthbert. Abigail. I begin the walk to the caravan site, pulling berries from the trees and keeping my face hidden behind my map. Cuthbert has been living for however long in a mobile home made from wood and plastic sheeting. Every one looks the same as the next and the last, the only difference being the numbers and the owner's desperate attempts to make their own house on wheels their home. Personal touches, pots of flowers and humorous signs reading 'I wish I was in Austria' lead me to the final building marked only with a 'No Strangers' sign on the front door. I knock hoping she remembers me.

'Who is it?' a man's voice asks.

'I'm looking for Abigail Cuthbert,' I say through the cheap wood of the door which opens on a man, middle-aged and slovenly.

He scratches his face and points over my shoulder.

'You have the wrong place, mate,' he says. 'You want seven.'

I follow his finger, nod and thank him for his help. He slams the door as I descend his steps. The mud is soft and dirty underfoot. House number seven has all the necessary touches of a woman, the pretty hanging baskets and the broken deck chairs outside. I wipe my feet on the matt reading 'HOME' and knock three times. No one comes running to the door with open arms and a wide smile. I knock again, harder and louder.

'Abigail?' I call.

'Who are you?'

I look around for the voice. I step back down into the mud and look up. A young girl's eyes stares down from the roof. She pulls herself further over the ledge and cocks her head at me. I say nothing.

'I'm not working today. Have you come for an art lesson?' she asks. 'Do I know you?'

I nod and ask her for her name.

'What's your name?' she says instead.

'Are you Abigail Cuthbert?'

She smiles a wide smile and shakes her head, 'Were you the one who found her?' she asks. 'When her parents died?'

I nod and shrug gently.

'I'll be right down,' she says, 'Wait right where you're standing.' She disappears. I let my feet sink into the mud.

The door opens and the girl beckons for me to come in. I stop in front of her and study her face. She has dark brown hair, cut short, and clear bronzed skin.

'You're not her,' I say.

'Come inside,' she replies, taking my arm.

'I'm looking for Abigail Cuthbert,' I feel myself repeating the words.

'For God's sake, you found her. Now come inside.'

We step into the caravan. The kitchen separates the living room and the small room with the single bed inside that must be where the girl sleeps.

'Would you like some coffee?' she asks, pointing at the table in the living room.

'No coffee, thank you.' I sit down as she tidies up the kitchen area. 'What's your name?' I ask.

She walks over to me, sitting on the other side of the table.

'She always said you'd come back for her. God. Right?'

I nod and ask, 'Where is she?'

'Abby died. She killed herself, four years ago next month.' The girl's eyes follow mine. She waits for me to reply.

'Why?' I ask.

'Why do you think?' she says back, meaner now, her voice is hurt and struggling.

'I'm sorry,' I tell her.

She shakes her head, 'It doesn't matter that you are. Here, I have this letter for you. That's all.'

She gets up and goes into the bedroom. There are drawings on the walls of the caravan and the table is covered with sketches and unfinished poems. I pick up a pencil outline of a young girl, no older than a child. There are only a few lines, but it could be of Cuthbert, it could be of anyone who looked like her. The girl comes back out and hands me an envelope. The word God has been scrawled across it in red pen. I look up at the girl.

'You can go now,' she says.

I hold up the picture.

'Can I have this?' I ask.

'No, it's not finished.'

I leave the caravan park with the letter stuffed into my trouser pocket. I walk down the track back to the river bank and my car. I try to remember Cuthbert's face and then I try to age it by six years. No matter what the letter says I cannot go back to work for Mr. Isles and he will not send for me, not after my repentance. Maybe I will stay in Durham for a while, find a cave, curl up and die. Maybe I should try to remember where I was born and raise up enough money to return there. Whatever happens now, I cannot go anywhere else.

I close the door of the rented car and break the seal of the envelope. The letter slides out into my hand.

'Godric?!' someone yells down the lane in a misplaced Scottish accent. Alec taps on my window. He opens the door and drags me out.

'What do you want, Alec?' He points vaguely at my hair

shirt. 'Who's the letter from, a former flame, a lost lover, a secret admirer, your mother?'

Two more Scotsmen stand at either side of Alec, who grins and nods his head to a rhythm only he is aware of.

'I'd like to read this,' I say. 'At least, before we discuss business.'

Alec snatches the letter from me. I grope a hand out at his face, but he sways backward and away. One of his heavies grabs my arm and pins me against the car. I struggle under the big man's weight, but there is no use in trying to free myself. The other man, larger than the one holding me, easily takes my neck in one of his hands.

'Quiet,' he tells me.

Alec prances around on his thick toes, reading Abigail's letter.

'Godric,' he laughs, 'I hope this letter finds you because, other than my name, it is the only thing I leave to this world…'

His voice trails off, his dancing becomes a frozen stance, the smile fades to concentration, but he continues to read. I gasp for breath and struggle to free one of my hands. Alec shakes his head and turns to me.

'What did you do, Godric?' he asks.

I gasp for air again.

'Frankie, don't hold him so hard.'

The larger man releases his grip on my neck. I breathe in and out, enjoying the oxygen and searching for an answer.

'Well, Godric, my old friend,' Alec says, punching me in the stomach, 'Looks like it's just one more thing you're gonna have to answer for.'

JUNGLE TEA
by ELIZA HEMINGWAY

THE lion tamer was at a debutante's party in the West End of London. I could see him near the liquor table with a drink in his hand, smiling slightly, a bored look on his face. He had on the latest design in burgundy tuxedos, no tie, just a shirt stud. The beautiful women squeezing up close were doing everything but stand on their hands to get his attention. The sight surprised me. The girl at my elbow, with a cleavage down to her navel and a smile as wide as the mouth of the Zambezi, said with a sigh, 'That's Thomas.' Her words rolled off her tongue as I imagined they might after she'd had great sex. She drooled over him as a tigress would over a baby lamb.

I was intrigued, I wanted to meet Thomas. Not that he was attractive – he wasn't. Quite the opposite. He was very short and bandy-legged with a badly-scarred face and long greasy black hair, but apparently these women adored him. I had to find out why. The woman at my side fell over herself to tell me.

Quite early on he realized he was ugly and without breeding. Not only did he not appeal to women, but he couldn't get an interesting job, and, besides which, small children didn't like

159

him. He was also regularly bitten by small dogs: a man outside the pack. Not exactly the kind of pedigree to get him the most out of life.

He could whine about his bad luck or make the best of things. He needed employment and thought, quite correctly as it turned out, that in the kind of job where people expected their lives to be in danger at some point they would rely on anyone, no matter what their rescuer's shortcomings. He scrounged about through newspaper ads and billboards – without much idea of what it was he was hoping to find – until he came across an interesting post that looked as though it might just suit.

On a board in the local library he stumbled on an ad for a Big Game Hunter: Man wanted to take excitable young women on safaris to Africa, experience not necessary but energy and a lust for life essential. He took the job, and discovered that lust was the operative word. After several bouts with protective lionesses he not only became more skilled at the job but also acquired another special kind of knowledge, one that gave him the advantage he needed to move him on a bit.

Under those magnificent stars of African nights, which aroused women into an overwhelming state to make love, Thomas was practically the only white man available for thousands of miles. This feisty little adventurer took advantage of the chance of a lifetime. It was on the job training, and in the process he gained pleasant and useful knowledge about what it is that women like. His escapades bagged him more than the skill needed for bringing down rampaging lions. He emerged from the experience a new man, one with confidence and style.

When it was no longer fashionable to shoot lions he took to game keeping and photography. But his ultimate success was as a lecturer on the circuit of universities and societies, and he even wrote a book, not mentioning any names. Jewellery-encrusted hostesses threw their arms around him with so much gusto he was often in more danger than he had been when he wrestled lion cubs. Not only did his mangled appearance captivate these ladies, but his soft voice purred out stories like no other man could, and they were true - well mostly anyway. And there was always gossip about his sexual stamina.

From his self-created animal university, he had adopted and fostered a cluster of characteristics that earned him a diploma of life. Ordinary guys were quietly jealous, and never figured it out but it was such a simple thing really: it wasn't what or who you were, or for that matter whom you knew, but it was how you stayed in control of the hunt that counted, and, if nothing else, Thomas was a born hunter. He also knew how to listen when women wanted to talk.

That was years ago. I didn't get to talk to him at the party that night in London – there were already too many women hanging on his arms – but I ran into him years later at a Vancouver art gallery opening in Canada. He had mellowed and was aging well and, even though his days of sexual encounters were fewer, or so he said, there was still an attractive air about him. He was in a dinner suit, similar to the one I had first seen him in, and as we talked he presented himself with as much sexuality as any six foot man, except he seemed to have shrunk somewhat from that time in London.

There was a scent of French perfume, his nails were manicured and I suspected his underwear and socks were probably made of silk. Throughout the opening he took my elbow to guide me around, got me drinks and listened attentively to any small thing I pointed out. He was a wonderfully charming escort, one I would have loved to have known better a few years back. Now it was too late. I am far too liberated for Thomas. There is an air of fustiness about him that doesn't appeal, something left over from another age and time when gigolos were popular and women dependent on them, even so I enjoyed pretending to be his date for the evening.

I know two Thomases, but now that I think about it there is a kind of nervousness about my other Thomas, something that might have to do with things that are off balance in his life. He emailed that he wanted to have tea. Now that's nice. It's the kind of thing any sensual lion tamer would have done. If he only shows up with one perfumed languorous rose the evening will be complete. I might be liberated, but my desire for nice gestures is still intact, and I love it when someone pampers me, as long as they are not phoney or pushy.

At three o'clock I'm in my closet knee-deep in clothes. I try on eight or nine outfits before I decide to wear the one I chose in the first place. I pull out my new high-heeled wedgies, push my toes into them and strut up the street to meet him.

I'm in a pencil thin black skirt with a side-split designed to expose my long legs, should I open it further for more effect? My blouse is black and white silk, striped like a tiger. Should I make it lower at the neck? Regardless, I'll get there first so I can choose a table for the right mood, one where I can sit with my back to the wall facing the door. I know Thomas well enough to suspect he won't care where he sits and the wrong choice of location can easily ruin an evening. We'll be finally seated, with the waitress gone and tea and whatever served, and I'll see how the game goes.

As I round the corner at the end of my street I see a police car outside the homeless shelter, which is a hangout for street people and junkies who often sprawl on the steps of their building waiting to say hello as people pass. They're no trouble really. I live downtown.

The suite was bought by accident. One morning, I opened the newspaper and fell in love with a name, Mermaid Wharf. The condo block is in Chinatown on Victoria's old docks, built on what was once the site for sheds and warehouses that housed opium and other bizarre eastern imports.

My one-room studio is fashionably small, like a lion cage I tell my friends, but it has everything I need and a three hundred and sixty degree roof top view of the harbour and the Empress Hotel that some people might kill for. I wake up and go to bed with smells of seawater; antique boats tooting and blowing every kind of whistle; the blinking neon lights of Chinatown always penetrating my blinds; motor bikes with illegal mufflers roaring loud; rowdy late-night pub-goers screaming out their joy at four in the morning; commercial garbage trucks arriving at five.

Chinatown is an enigma. Its painted dragon gate looms in the near distance as I saunter towards Swans' restaurant. Red, black, and yellow storefronts remain the same as they were the day they were put up. I indulge myself and linger a little longer. I like to listen to wind chimes jingling their melodies to scare away unfriendly spirits. A smell of dumplings and tobacco smoke reminds me that I'm hungry. I head off to meet Thomas. At four I sink into a seat. I don't order yet because I know he'll want to do that. I have a bad feeling about this get-together. I concentrate on vibrations; memories from times in the past when we have met. I am sure he has slotted me in, I am an item scheduled between other appointments.

Swans' pub is a local watering hole, a five-minute stroll from Mermaid Wharf and a nice place for tourists to stumble into on their safari through town. The sun is hot through the glass wall at my back. In the steady heat and dusty drone of late afternoon small slim jean-clad Chinese girls giggle through their frosty tall teas and leave. Big-bellied Americans come next, grab the same seats the girls just slid out of, order double hamburgers and jugs of beer, gorge themselves and leave. And there is still no Thomas. This is the third time he has asked me out for tea, and not shown up.

A smiling man with a beard sitting nearby sends out signals. I suspect he hopes I am going to talk, eventually to him. At what time do I call it quits? I decide that over an hour's wait in a crowded harbour bar is more than long enough for any full-breasted woman. At five-fifteen I am back at Mermaid Wharf.

There's an email: *I'll be late, see you at 4.45.* He seldom uses the phone, even though I have an answering service. I'm a good sport so don't mind a game of hide and seek with Thomas a while longer, besides which I am all dressed up with nowhere to go. I head back to Swans' again, even though it is already past the time he said he would be there. On the way I pass David sunning himself on the concrete steps outside the street shelter.

The doorway faces west, the only part of the building exposed to the evening warmth just before the sun goes down. He is a nice looking blond-haired man, a young junkie who lives on hand-outs and stays here when he has pan-handled enough money for a room. I always say hello. He seems intelligent, and he likes to talk back when he's not doped up. When he is, he lies on the steps with his face to the sky and smiles to himself about… I never pry, but often wonder how he lost his direction. Some of my friends give him money and one of them cooks him special dinners, but not me, I don't. With my kind of sensibility I'd end up adopting him. Other men come out of their small rooms to sit as well; it's their social hour, a buzzing ring round the bottom of a monkey tree.

When Thomas finally arrives he'll probably just say sorry, I was feeding a girlfriend's cats; or something like that. Which is exactly what happens. He has already told me he hates restrictions of any kind, preferring to roam loose and free. Punctuality tends to tie him down. I wonder why I'm involved at all. He will eventually push too far, force me to a point when enough is enough. I could finish this with one of those outbursts I'm famous for. An expert at the dramatic exit line, I can see myself getting up from our table to go towards the door with my sultry voice carrying back over my shoulder: Oh, by the way – a hand across my brow, the other stretched dramatically in front – I'm leaving for Madagascar immediately; start without me, this might take a while.

Meanwhile, I'm back at Swans' in a different seat and he still isn't here. Half an hour goes by and he finally breezes in, wearing the same brown-checked shirt as the last time we met. I hate brown and I detest checks. With all the colours there are in the world why dress so drably? Maybe he needs to blend in with the chairs and tables so he won't be seen; won't be caught by whichever human hunters are out tonight. His brown thinning hair is slicked down and he is scrubbed-clean and in a hurry. As I look up he seems surprised to see me. He catches his breath as a lion might that has been running through trees until it stumbles across this clearing to come face to face with me by accident.

Why am I here? Oh, great lovers of the world where are you? I would love a dinner partner who can whisper entrancing ideas and tell me stories. My mind is on the other Thomas. I wonder why I can't have the best of both worlds; my independence and a great lover who is dedicated only to me.

Eating, like love is a passionate affair. I select food carefully, imbibe its subtle flavours and look at its combination of colors and exotic shapes. I delight in the way asparagus tips and nasturtium petals loll across the whiteness of my plate. Eye indulgence is best when done slowly, preferably with a western sun setting in the distance.

From Swans' there is often an overwhelming orangey-misty-purple dying of the day. I imagine it to be similar to nights over African pampas grass. This one reaches across the blue metal Johnson Street swing-bridge to glisten its colors through the window onto my raw vegetables. I pick up orange carrots in my fingers, put my head back and drop them over my tongue. They are gems from a jewel box from King Solomon's mines.

Thomas eats because he's hungry, and then he gorges fast. He orders a plate of curried shrimp and scrapes it all down. With his arms curled around this huge platter to protect it from marauders, he scoffs with an open mouth while I talk. He's a starving animal, one that at any moment could lick up the sauce. As he stuffs home the last forkful I know he's one step away from losing me. When the waitress comes to remove the dirty dishes he finally leans on his arms to look into my face as if he has just realized I am here. By now I am a little less interested, and in a way sorry I ever met him.

I lean in to tell him about my other Thomas, the lion tamer, thinking it might help, maybe bring about some finesse. His head goes back to send a roar of laughter through the bar. He says he'll tell George. Am I missing something here? Who is George? A twitter starts behind me in the jungle, birds being disturbed. I look around at the eating going on in particular spaces. They are parrots and sparrows on branches in a mango tree – multicoloured, flaunting their finery, pecking away at their Brazil nuts and bananas – and I hear how his roar has made them rustle. The noise swells, as it often does in a crowd when one of the species talks louder than the others. It will fall back in a while to a quieter tone.

He can't pick up my sensitivity, we will never connect. And here comes that feeling again, as though a zookeeper just gave me – an intruder – the heave-o out the gate. As I said, I'm a quickie on his fast game-sheet. I should have some guts, maybe stand up and smoke him: Bang! Bang you're gone!

All this, but still I don't give up. It is the time of night when mates collide, the first part of the darkness. I parade my silken sexuality in front of him, a female out to attract her male. My ten thousand-dollar pearls drop between my breasts. I lift them to rub across my lips while I dip a silver-tipped fingernail into my lemon soda to gently nudge the ice around. We are male and female drinking at sunset as the serious night chase is about to start in earnest, before the darkest part of the night comes.

My topaz and diamond ring is caught in the last light of this Chinese evening. I am a coral snake; my tongue darts out to touch the sparkle. I adore jewellery, heck I love anything that's beautiful. He stares at the softness of my breasts over the edge of my blouse as though he senses something. But his last chance is closing fast. *Don't be slow, Thomas*, I whisper inside my heart, *capture me while you can, let me be your lioness. I am near to escape and if you let me go you will never know what you missed.*

He asks what I like doing best. It's a lazy question from an indolent male who has just eaten too much and now sits with an uncomfortable stomach. He needs me to entertain him. He's curious about my life before him. I lower my gaze from the

Oriental red sun, caught, a fallen kite among the condos on the Esquimalt side of the gorge, the other end of the bridge. With all the sexuality of the female of the species I look into his eyes. He stretches himself, tenses his muscles as though he is ready to conquer every living thing I have ever been in contact with. Maybe it's a way for him to discover his own prowess. Similar to the lion tamer, he may have something he needs to do to make himself more important, but what and to whom? It's a guy thing I decide.

I splash around among my drink bubbles while I think. I could give him a response that he would be comfortable with but don't want things to be too easy.

Love making love, I say and it's the truth. The answer makes him giggle. It's a gal thing, but he doesn't know that. I lift my swizzle stick from my drink to slide it dripping across my lips, a sensual move done deliberately to get his attention. Does nothing work here? This old brown lion is past his prime.

He finishes his safe flirt with the waitress and we leave. He reaches for a hug as I turn to cross the road, but not this time I decide, I don't want him to squeeze me with his bloated stomach and I definitely don't want him to kiss me with those scrunched shrimp between his teeth. We'll keep in touch he says, yet I know I won't, and he won't phone because he's scared I might say no, and that will leave him hanging in silence on the other end of the line, caught out. He'll email to entice me when he thinks enough time has elapsed, but it will be too late and I'll be gone. His trap will be empty.

A sharp breeze across a street grating blows swirls of grit through the slits in my skirt. I am a film star in hot Los Angeles. I clutch my silver purse to my breasts and don't look back as I mince past the tea and rice stores on my way home to Mermaid Wharf. The last darkness of the evening has started, the time of night when major players come out. Their games will last until just before dawn. This is a dangerous time; soon it will be the hour of the wolf, not a good moment to hang around.

This is Chinatown. The smells have changed. I try not to inhale the dankness of strange drugs, try not to listen to the screechy women's voices jangling in rhythm to a background of instruments with one or two strings, and I turn my eyes away from lips enlarged with colour, hair lacquered and pinned. These are girls at the glowing street corners. Chinatown is where everyone meets. This is the last time I shall safari out to meet Thomas.

As I turn the corner towards Mermaid Wharf the drug addicts are still loafing on the festering-dirt steps, but now an ambulance waits as well as the police car. One person is gone. I shrug it off as I slink almost noiselessly by. Such is the way of the night in a downtown jungle. David, while I had tea with Thomas, overdosed and died. One person gone, tomorrow another will take his place.

THE LAST SMOKER
by NICK MONTGOMERY

I **CAME** into possession of the last box of cigarettes in the world while I was clearing a drawer in my brother's bureau. He had died six days earlier of liver failure, and it occurred to me that the patches of exposed wood on the bureau top, where the veneer had peeled, and then been stained by spilt rum, were of the same fake tan orange as the skin of his face during those final days. 'Death rattle' suggests a brief, violent sound, while the gentle garglings I came to know in his hospital cubicle had, for me anyway, resolved into a soothing musical motif, ornamented by the reassuring, quantized precision of the bleeping and buzzing machines and instruments surrounding his bed.

It was a box of two hundred Lucky Strike, buried in a drawer beneath a dozen or so dusty sheets of Paracetamol and some papers covered in half legible scrawlings, some in Latin, some in Ancient Greek, with some minute annotations in English. Lucky Strike had been my brand of choice some twenty years earlier when I was a student, but the name and packet design were now a little violated by the clumsy irony created by this new archaeological context. They were a 'lucky strike' in the all too literal way that exposes the tastelessness and absence of plausibility that so often smears and coarsens reality. I found myself grieving for the red simplicity of Winston or the clear, brash honesty of Marlboro. I wasn't about to look a gift horse in the mouth, however, and my squeamishness quickly modulated into the controlled ecstasy of any miraculous excavation. I had found water in the desert or the broken head of Ozymandias. Even this treasure, though, was doomed, I knew, to be consumed, and the shiny cellophane wrapping already spoke of loss. A petal dropped from one of the miniature red roses my brother had planted in a teapot on top of the bureau. I retreated to my bedroom with my find to ponder and plan, aghast at the hapless irony of the discovery and the crass symbolism of the falling petal

In my room I had two precious boxes that I kept on top of my bookcase. One, a shoebox, contained my own dog-ends, each with about a quarter of an inch of tobacco intact. Also in this box were two packets of green Rizla papers, a rolling machine and fifteen slimline filters. The second box must, I think, have been designed for pot-pourri. It was of a hard wood, with star-shaped and hexagonal holes carved out of the lid. It looked Turkish or Moroccan. Inside were fourteen roll-ups made from former contents of the first box.

I was faced with a dilemma, a choice; to save the Lucky Strike until I had smoked all of the dog-end roll-ups, or to treat myself to one packet of my immaculate discovery. I went to the kitchen and made a pot of strong dark coffee. The aroma fought off the lingering smell of urine that had characterized the flat since the beginning of my brother's incontinence and had seen the visits of old friends become briefer and more infrequent until they ceased altogether. I took the milk, sugar, our best china cup and the coffee pot to my bedroom and sat down on my favourite large cushion in front of our antiquated portable TV. I un-wrapped the box of Lucky Strike, opened a packet, and looked at the perfect arrangement of white filter heads. It put me in mind of a mosaic floor, but bleached of colour.

'You only live once,' I said aloud, taking out one cigarette and carefully pushing the others back into place. 'I'll smoke this for you.'

How I came to be the last smoker in the world is really a matter for historians to work out. What I know of causes, processes, religious and economic changes, substitution of crops, global agricultural strategy, new trading and commercial structures, national and regional variations and trends, the pace and intricacies of the cessation of the practice of smoking tobacco, are inadequate for me to make any authoritative remarks on the phenomenon. Suffice to say, it was a velvet global revolution, with no bloodshed, no draconian laws passed, no catastrophic event or medical innovation. Abstaining from smoking possibly started as one aspect of the health religion, in my eyes an unwholesome, and in some cases fanatical body fundamentalism, with the subtext that true believers could not die. Or perhaps it was merely a kind of fad, an affectation, a species of self-definition, which then became a fashion whose chief accessory was an absence, then a blinkered collective obsession. There was a sudden surge, an unstoppable momentum, a tidal wave, a flash flood, a forest fire, an avalanche, a pyroclastic flow. It became a virus, a fatal epidemic, a plague of abstention. The desire to smoke simply withered; smoking slowly ceased even to be a topic of conversation. Giving up smoking meant living forever. In some parts the belief was widely held that all diseases were smoking related. For a while there were subversive web-sites which temporarily provided a black market supply for those perverse enough to persist with the habit, but a decline of site hits and a dissipation of interest saw these internet outlets lapse. Ashtrays became obsolescent desirable ornaments in some homes, collectors' items, while tobacco pipes took over from horse brasses in many rural public houses. Any further explanation on my part would be insupportable speculation

Kiss and suck, kiss and suck.

Breathe and blow.

I drank the strong coffee, smoking three consecutive ciga-rettes and remembered my brother's throwaway remark that, 'Life without fags would be an EE Cummings poem that never ended; completely devoid of punctuation.'

I flattered him at the time with comparisons to Wilde and Dorothy Parker. He drank the compliments greedily. I thought of Humphrey Bogart and Lauren Bacall, and all the great celluloid smoking moments, and was, for a while, overwhelmed by a vision of a smokeless world, adrift, aimless and gutless, and a rich cultural history casually denuded of meaning.

The sun was going down and a few wintry rays made golden shapes of the nicotine stains on my window, intricate abstract forms, resolving into grotesque faces, fronds of seaweed, or fantastic extinct flowers. The smoke from my third cigarette twisted and curled or hung in stubborn clouds in the dying light. The souls of the dead were restless in my room and reluctant to leave. I put the three dog-ends into my shoebox.

Wandering now back into my brother's room with a fresh coffee and my large aluminium ashtray, I looked at some of the things a dead person leaves behind. There were two books open on the bureau, *The Odyssey* and *Swallows and Amazons*. The wardrobe was open, bulging with clothes, most of which he never wore. An old plastic urine bottle lay on its side just under the bed, along with a selection of slippers, socks, and shoes; including the size twelve light brown brogues he had bought to accommodate his swollen feet. The duvet was crumpled as if someone had got up in a hurry, late for work. The empty wheelchair looked especially forlorn, embarrassed by its redundancy. I found myself sitting down in it to keep it company. I moved my hand along the armrest, pausing on a patch of dried blood, a trace of the spewed haemorrhage which had brought the ambulance and the invasion of the green uniformed paramedics.

'I'm touching my own Y chromosome,' I thought, indulging my ignorance about human biology.

The chair creaked in a familiar way as I reached to the floor to pick up the plate-sized ashtray. I lit a fourth Lucky Strike and again said aloud, 'I'll smoke this for you.'

As I smoked I explored ways of prolonging my smoking life. I could lengthen the dog-ends, but I was low on Rizla papers; I could smoke half a cigarette at a time; I could stop altogether and inhabit the safe knowledge that my supply would never diminish; I could kill the days by sitting motionless in front of the TV; I could smoke as if there were no tomorrow. I knew stopping altogether was out of the question, so I stared full in the face the inevitable moment when there would be no tobacco left.

Somebody, sometime had to be the last smoker in the world. The idea of a date with destiny, a place in history was momentarily seductive, but almost immediately overpowered by the question, 'Why me?'

What was going to fill all that endless space and time? What will I do when I stub out the last cigarette in the world? And will I have the right?

JAMES

by KIRSTEN BERGEN

THE jacket he was repairing lay forgotten in his lap as he absently fingered the button to be sewed on. His gaze had strayed to the grimy window and the world outside and he had let his mind wander, take flight:

Feather light wings span the sky; some mystic white giant of the air. Free and wild against the burning turquoise blue. A heavy, dusty grey covering creeps forward, encircling, ensnaring and enslaving. The beautiful majestic white beings are reduced, humiliated, assimilated until they succumb. Totally. Annihilated. The murky, dull, ugly blanket covers the earth, suffocating light and happiness, pressing down, emitting a low growl. Melting into the belching soot, the retching fumes and the vomiting smoke, the camouflage of industrial gloom and capitalist ugliness is perfect and complete. The dream shattered; peace gone. The spark of life is nothing but a faint, dying glow. Waves of doubt pulling down, drowning in emptiness, energy and will sucked from the soul…

But he won't give up. He won't die. He will find a way. There must be a way. With a deep sigh he tore his eyes from the window, his face set in grim resolution.

Never let them know what you think, what you feel. Always keep your guard up. Maybe his sigh was too loud, maybe his body heaved too much as he exhaled, maybe he had betrayed himself. You're not alone. You're never alone. There are always eyes prying and ears hearing. Apart from that, there were three other people in the small workroom.

Not long now. He knew it. One way or another he would be gone. Either the way they planned, or the way he chose. Maybe a miracle would happen and he would wake up and realize this was all just a bad dream. But then it would be a very vivid bad dream which had lasted far too long.

The fingers of claustrophobia curled around his heart. How he longed to be out, to be free and roaming, to be able to relax and stop hiding, stop running from the invisible enemy. Even if it was only out to that desolate, dreary wasteland visible from the small, grimy window and even if it was only for an hour. Anything. Just a short respite.

How he longed to see his family, his friends, his little daughter. She would be five now. He had missed her first steps, her first words. Could she say 'Daddy'? Did she know who he was? Would she even care? How long had it been since he had seen anyone? Did anyone still care about him, try to visit him? Would he ever know? Sometimes they told him that he wasn't allowed visitors. Sometimes they said they had turned his loved ones away. Sometimes they said no one had asked to see him for months. No letters, no messages, nothing.

A few beads of sweat broke out on his forehead and his rough, scratchy shirt suddenly started clinging to his body. Get a grip. Calm down. Come on, grip it. His commands to himself sounded panicky, desperate. Slowly he calmed, slowly his heart stopped racing, slowly he could turn around and face the others.

The guards were playing their favourite game with the inmates. 'What do you miss most here?' The typical question. So seemingly innocent. Such a trap. So dangerous. Almost anything you said could and would be used against you. To taunt you, haunt you, tear you apart. He had learned fast. It was his turn.

'What do you miss most here, James?'

'Whiskey' he said automatically, the lie now coming easily from his lips.

The lie. All his life he had fought for justice, truth, transparency and honesty. And now he told the same lies every day. His whole life was a farce, a lie.

'Whiskey,' he said a little more forcefully, making it sound sincere and urgent. 'I really miss the whiskey.'

The mocking laughter. What did it matter. He hated whiskey, had never liked the hard stuff. Only the odd cold beer, never any hard liquor. He had seen what devils alcohol could awaken and had often suffered at the hands of the possessive demons. Never, he had sworn to himself, never will I touch the stuff. He had been ten years old.

He knew what would happen tonight. The usual. A couple of guards would station themselves outside his cell with a bottle of whiskey and one glass too many; already poured, but out of reach. They would spend hours there engaging him in meaningless banter getting drunker and drunker as the minutes slipped into hours. And still the one glass would be pointedly placed directly in front of him, just out of his reach and never offered. They would find it hilarious, taunting him as the drunkenness took its grip. Eventually they would leave, stagger down the hallway, whooping and shouting on the way to their quarters to sleep and wake up in the morning in the unforgiving embrace of a bad hangover, leaving the glass behind to torment him – or so they believed.

It was a small inconvenience. It was something to be tolerated. And heck, he sometimes also gleaned important snippets of information from them. Someone had asked after him. A message for him had been intercepted and he would know which prisoner to seek out for the much longed for news. Carefully, imperceptibly, innocently approach him, find a way to talk unobserved and then quickly disappear again.

Such events were much more preferable to the ordeals the unwary went through. He had heard of stories of abuse, beatings and even open torture. He was thankful that he seemed to be taboo, that he was spared. There was nothing he could say or do anyway to stop it. Consoling the victims after was a sure ticket to reprisals. How he hated it here.

He had learnt fast. At the beginning he had said he missed his family and friends, that he wished he could have more visits. The agony and heartbreak that had led to.

'Hey James, we rang to see if anyone wanted to visit you, but no one cared,' or 'Your wifey came last week, but we told her to leave, said you didn't want to see her any more.'

Sometimes they would wave a letter just out of his reach, tear it open, read it greedily to themselves and make sordid comments, then rip it up while he could do nothing, just watch. Sometimes they would come by handing out the post, stopping at his cell and making a great show of looking for a letter for him, then say that no one had written, no one cared, they had all abandoned him, forgotten him, and then carry on to the next cell saying loudly,

'Hey, you got three letters this week, lucky you. People still care about you and haven't forgotten you.'

He was a victim of the system. Since they had come to power so many had fallen. Many had given up to save their lives, to save the ones they loved. He had been one of the handful who couldn't renounce his beliefs. He couldn't turn his back on the truth. They may have squashed freedom of expression, but they could never destroy freedom of thought.

He had managed to survive in semi freedom for a year, writing short articles, commentaries and editorials under a pseudonym. He had to use a pseudonym for the sake of his family, to try to keep them safe. He hid by day and moved about cautiously by night. He went to small, informal gatherings to discuss what was happening and what could be done to rein in the gross floutings of the law, the increasing iron grip of power of the megalomaniacs. His abode had changed almost as often as he changed his clothes. But seeing as he only owned three threadbare suits and five worn shirts, that hadn't been nearly as often as he would have liked.

Then it happened. The raid. They came in broad daylight, broke the door in. The sickening groan and splintering of the wood as it crashed in and came part way off its hinges, hanging limply, a broken barricade. They smashed the windows after they barged in. They went through the small house systematically ramming their batons into the window panes. They had kicked the furniture over. The simple yet elegant wooden corner table Ira's husband had given her as a wedding present was overturned and broken as if it had been nothing more than a matchstick. That was the one prized possession of hers other than the photograph of them together in front of the registry office which hung in the simple metal frame above the table. They tore that down, smashed the glass and ripped the photo up. They knew what hurt most and they did their deeds cruelly, ruthlessly, gleefully.

They had ransacked the house, taking the precious few items of any value with them. They beat Ira. She was 73, but they didn't care, they just beat her. He never found out if she had survived. He was taken away together with the two others. The last thing he had heard was a faint whimper from the broken, frail heap in the corner, the heap that was the once proud, strong, indomitable Ira.

Arthur committed suicide the day the verdict was announced. They were branded traitors, dissidents, terrorists accused of plotting to overthrow the state. They were held responsible for the explosions, the acts of vandalism, the power cuts, the mass lootings and the freezing of the bank accounts. Anything that could be invented or blamed on them, no matter how incredible or impossible, was. The accusations ran to over 200 pages. 200 pages of lies. Arthur couldn't take it. They had been deserted, abandoned, left to flounder, to drown. He had decided to die rather than face a life of disgrace in prison. Sometimes James could understand his decision, even if it was an unspeakable crime to take your own life.

'Get back to work,' a guard growled from just behind his elbow.

With an effort James pulled his attention back into the present, back to the meaningless task he had been set. This was the fourth week in a row he'd been on the line. Sewing buttons onto the prison uniforms. Mountains of jackets needing buttons replaced. How did so many buttons come off, he wondered? He had heard a rumour that one work team spent its days simply tearing the buttons off jackets to provide work for another team to sew them back on. It was a rumour that hadn't been confirmed though. And rumours are dangerous.

Picking up the jacket which had fallen neglected on his lap, he pulled the thread tight, sewed over the button the reglementary four times then wound the thread round the button and anchored the stitching securely on the back before biting the thread off. They weren't allowed scissors or knives. Biting the threads made threading the needle difficult. In fact, the whole chore was difficult because the needle was so blunt you could hardly get it through the rough, canvas textured material.

He was always on the sewing team when the seasons were most alluring. It was neither too hot nor too cold out. Most days the sun played hide and seek amongst the white fluffy clouds which sailed lightly overhead. Sometimes though the weather was bad, like today. It had started raining and got cooler. There was a storm in the air.

In the summer he had to work in the quarry. The sun beat down relentlessly, the heat oppressive pushing him almost physically down to the ground. The white of the stone in the quarry was reflected as an intense, piercing, blinding light. The rhythmic chinking of the picks on the stone echoed dully in his ears. Bodies bent, burdened by the heat, the back breaking work, the exhaustion, the hunger, the thirst. Sweat glistening on the bare backs and arms, running down the white dust in rivulets, blinding the eyes. The air was almost too hot to breathe, and each breath filled your lungs with dust, stifling you, choking you. Fourteen hours a day. Six days a week. Permanent aching muscles, never ending headache, throat searing. When evening came and the prisoners trudged heavily back to the compound three kilometres away the two thoughts uppermost in everyone's minds were: water, bed. They were too tired and broken to worry much about hunger, or anything else.

Winter was spent waist deep in near freezing water, rain pelting down when they were lucky, wind chilling them to the bone. Winter time was for cleaning the canal and the river. Dozens of shivering, pale ghosts plunging their arms into the murky muck to pull up discarded shoes, tyres, bicycle parts and unthinkable gunk. Teeth chattering so hard that it was impossible to hear anything else, snow often swirling around them, drowning out all other sound, making each man a lone, forsaken island in the cold. Out of touch and out of reach of any one else, icy fingers slowly clawing at their bodies and souls. Even their minds seemed to freeze. Numbed into submission, working like mindless robots. If any thoughts did pass fleetingly through their heads, they were of warmth, dryness and food. And even those thoughts were pushed out of their consciousness as quickly as possible. They knew that a lukewarm shower, a set of still damp clothes and a thin, but thankfully warm bowl of broth or porridge waited for them. That seemed like heaven to look forward to. Had they really fallen so far?

Spring and autumn were the only times they had enough to eat, were neither too hot nor too cold and felt in any way comfortable. It was also the only time they wanted to be outside the confines of the prison, and the only time it was denied them. Except for the brief half hour out in the courtyard surrounded by the hulking grey walls just before sunrise and at sundown, just after the sun had sunk below the horizon but before full dark had settled in.

The hours dragged on. He occupied himself with repeating the names of capital cities by continent. Then he listed all the names of local flora. He went through all of the presidents, prime ministers and dignitaries, recapping on their lives and their activities. A detailed biography for each one mapped in his mind, meticulously filed and pulled out as and when needed. Then he went on to reflect on what he had been fighting for. What were the facts? What were the lies? What were rumours and what could be set in concrete? Where was the black and white? Where were the grey areas? What had they renounced? What would they need to renounce in the future?

Listing the events in the lead up to the mass arrests he suddenly pulled himself up short and chided himself. The ration quota had been modified on the ninth, before curfews had been extended on the eleventh. He mustn't forget the details. Forgetting the details or getting them mixed up would jeopardize their whole fight. He needed to know everything for when he got out. He would get out. He had to. He had been sentenced to three life sentences.

The all too familiar, treacherous, paralysing panic began to creep around his heart: would he ever get out? Not now, now is not the time to panic, he told himself. Keep it for tonight, when it's dark, when no one can see, no one can know. His face became an expressionless mask again as he picked up the next button to sew.

NEW ORLEANS
by DAVID BRECKENRIDGE

I MOVED to New Orleans in my late teens from a one-bedroom basement apartment in Mormon Salt Lake City. Fled out of boredom. To me the city was bragging, boasting the highest crime rate in all America.

Stepped off of that bus with no preconceptions. Heard a drill starting up, trying to be subtle and twist things into my memory for the first ten minutes after my arrival.

In the animal world they call this imprinting, and in truth imprinting is just this really fake sensation, an instinct in a world where logic prevails. It's this feeling like everything you are seeing is suddenly important.

As it was stuck with staples from advertisements, flyers for lost cats and lost dogs, I do remember that telephone pole well enough.

And next to the pole was a total stranger, East Indian man in a black turtleneck with puffy hair.

He had a tab just like a file-folder floating above his bran-muffin face, a sign that said: 'UNAM!'

And the whitest-looking white gal wearing everything a Prosumer should have been wearing standing there with her boy right beside her. I still remember him being a bit mechanical, the way he blinked. He was just that breed of man.

'MISTER AND MISSES ORAM,' read the sign that he didn't bother to even hold up.

And then there was middle-aged Richard hoisting up the sign: 'NEED A ROOM?' in a plaid golf-shirt and well-creased khakis.

His hands shaking, his face red, the way he held that sign was advertising in itself. He was newborn-pink all over beneath the weight of a paper billboard.

One thing I'd never given much thought to before I met Richard was rental policy at nursing homes.

When an old person, head bowed from life, comes to the front desk to get booked in, they pay first and last month's rent, the same as everywhere else.

Now the thing about last month is that last month is obviously unspecified when you're so close to the end, and so only a few tenants manage to give their two-month notice before moving on. The landlord, in this case Richard, has to rush around filling rooms and never knowing when another vacancy will spring.

When I was nineteen I moved to New Orleans and lived at Pineview Retirement Inn. It was home because home was cheap and smelt like death and Grandparents.

Pineview was grey-brick on a side street with one tree. The entrance had multiple security cameras and a pass code system either side of a hefty aluminium door I couldn't have opened if I were old. The hallways were all lit overhead, felt industrial, felt long with a tiresome orange carpet pattern going on below my feet.

Room four-eleven became my room, painted sterile teal, the color of hospital gowns, the color of chlorinated pool water.

Standing still in the dark I could hear my neighbour's clock ticking. It must have been hung right up against the wall.

Potted by the window above my single-mattress bed was a flower bulb.

'Whose plant does this belong to?' I asked Richard, who had agreed on carrying all my luggage.

'Oh that daft'dill?' he said, dropping my two cases. 'Technically it belongs to no one at all... And of all the folks, it has been here the longest. Yep, at least eighty years... And it just comes with the room. Beautiful when it flowers.'

'Outlives them all,' I whispered.

'What was that?' asked Richard.

'Nothing. I was just whispering something to myself, that's all,' I said. 'Just whispering something, that's all.'

I stood on my toes to get a good look out the window, the drizzle coming down on a vegetable garden in my new cramped-in backyard.

I would be out to raid it later and routinely for carrots and tomatoes, turnips and yam, lettuce and chives.

Richard was a nervous man. He stuttered and hung around but left as fast as he could, whamming the door with the misplaced frustration that sometimes can account for such clumsiness, I do believe.

Inhaled the boredom and history of room four-eleven, hearing the echo of dead people's last words, raspy little tones still bouncing around like flies against the ceiling, moths against the overhead light bowls and streaks of sandy white paints.

As contagious as old people are, symptoms of laziness, cake, kittens, television viewing and lethargy... I had to remind myself that I was not retired or dying, crippled or mentally deficient... I needed to fight and find work, invent credentials, bribe references and write letters from them to me. I took days off from being unemployed to just bake and hang out in the Gossip Lounge of the fourth floor, where I schemed for the more long-term.

Did some extensive note-taking there in that low-ceilinged lounge with too many couches, one huge television. All words came around twice thanks to an echo, either human or spatial, in the room. Nothing got passed my note pad.

Everyone there had life insurance and a will filled out but nobody really wanted to talk about that with a nineteen year-old, however it seemed like reasonable chit-chat to inquire if they were proud Grandparents, or not.

'Yes I have two of them,' said Rachel. 'Thomas and... Anyway they're both boys, but enough about them! Haven't been to visit me in nine years. *Nine years!* You know what they are? They're punks! And I mean it.'

She waved her finger in between her myopic pupils, each as tiny as a pen's tip.

She pinched her eyebrow between her thumb and forefinger, making a ring.

'The younger one, he has a hole right through there like an animal!' she sighed and deflated on the couch. '...Like an animal!'

I took note of the tan-line on her ring finger. Widower. Cheap ruby on the next.

'I know what you mean,' I said.

High-price cologne, hundred-dollar bottle, but she talked about having a good relationship with her younger brother, probably on the will.

After sorting out everyone I met in order of financial standings I went back to my room. I decided who was worth baking apple crumble for:

Lonely people and especially lonely people with money. Company was the more important commodity for people of such age, anyway.

It seemed to me that the generation gap was merely a difference in importance, a difference in commodities and a difference in priorities.

The young want money to spend or stockpile; the old have

money stockpiled but want company and youth...

The solution seemed too obvious and worked symbiotically.

Nine o'clock the walls began to snore in around me.

I walked out of my room barefoot to find some white sugar, met a few die-hards in the television room, no one that could really have helped.

'We don't have none,' was the dismissal. 'Why you want sugar now, anyway? Bad for yo' health, young man!'

'What are you jaunting to the store for?' Tom asked.

'White sugar,' I said. 'If no one can help me out...'

'You're a white what?' asked Melinda.

'White sugar,' I said.

I just bit my lip and nodded, started to step backward out of the door, and how old Melinda, she glared at me then... like an enemy and I had no idea why.

Even the TV was put on mute. All I could hear was feedback from Melinda's hearing aid. The mood was very heavy to breathe and it all radiated from her lethargically lethal eyebrows. Melinda's face was an old cobra with saggy fangs – you could tell that a long time ago it could have been pretty intimidating.

I shrugged that off. Figured they were exaggerating. Sugar's not that bad for you, is it?

Came back with a pound of it tucked in under my jacket.

Using my oven's timer I slept and baked all at the very same time.

Elmira was at my door at six thirty the next morning shaking from arthritis and knocking with her cane.

'Yes?' I rubbed my eyes.

She scanned my half-naked body, my black briefs.

'You white supremacist, be gone wit' yah!' Elmira said. 'So be it 'den, man across from the fire extinguishah!'

With the large teal eraser head of her cane she collapsed my chest and I fell straight back into bed.

The door swung closed on her angry expression that would've once been pretty scary, and I laughed out loud.

'White sugar!' I shouted. 'White sugar!'

And then I understood Melinda's misunderstanding. Went to the store for white sugar, came back a white supremacist.

George stopped me in the hall on my way to deliver the first apple crumble to Misses Drydell.

'Look! It's the racist!' he shouted, four inches away from my face and no one else in the halls.

'Ohhhh, do you know me from television? Number 48! Catch me Thursdays and Sundays on channel three. I'm a cyclist... Got a race coming up, too... Good day!'

Mrs. Drydell was so pleased with my apple crumble that she wouldn't let me leave without seeing a bird go in for a bird bath outside of her floor-to-ceiling window.

The birdbath was just a bowl, a plastic replica of some antique, metal-worker's craft with pieces of price tag still stuck on it...

'Isn't it something?' she asked.

I didn't look very hard.

'In deed it is,' I replied.

I ate a piece with Mrs. Drydell as she talked about baking. She was a tough critic, but I think I passed.

About half-way through the bowl, a yellow, orange and red pigeon splashed down into the bird bath outside. I was at first puzzled, then I laughed and laughed more hysterically than any old geezer, spraying crumble onto the rug. Mrs. Drydell laughed with me as the bird pulled itself out of the water, now covered in purple dye.

'Look for them about the downtown area,' she said. 'Drydell's birds... They come in a variety of colors.'

Getting back to room four-eleven an old man was at my door trying to peak the wrong way through the peak-hole.

'You a psychoanalyst?' his pizza-dough lips blurted out like an obnoxious, confused odour.

I shrugged and gave it some silence.

'You bet cha' I'm a cyclist,' I said. 'So come on in... Sit

yourself down.'

Ten seconds into amateur hypnosis using soap-on-the-rope for a fob watch, Greg's cave nostrils were snoring on my couch and I got back to baking in the kitchen. A few hours and a few apple crumbles later, coming back through the living room and there was no more of the hypnotized stranger. He had put on his slippers and gone.

That was fine with me. I delivered the last four apple crumbles before lights out. Stole fresh veggies out the garden and just managed to nap before my waking.

'So,' said Greg as I rubbed my eyes at six in the morning.

'So...'

He was grinning wide.

'So...' he said. 'What'd we find out yesterday?'

' ... You went to sleep, man,' I said. 'So... Nothing.'

He bit down on his lip but I could tell part of him had expected me to answer that way. It had seemed too logical to admit it to himself, however.

'So...' said Greg. 'I got a good night sleep... Had a double-double this morning... Would you mind we give it another go?'

I opened the door and put Greg to sleep on the couch using soap-on-a-rope. I too went back to sleep in my bed for a few more hours.

The scraggly old man became a permanent fixture in my room, room four eleven, because we never managed to get past the first few steps of the hypnosis procedure without him dozing off, which was all the better seeing as I didn't know what came next, anyway.

'Maybe you'd like to just tell me what's wrong?' I asked him, finally. 'If there ever was anything wrong, that is... and we'll go from there?'

Greg ranked high in the wealth plot of Pineview.

Unfortunately for me he had strong ties with Grandchildren who visited him every second Sunday afternoon. He put them to work looking for snails in the vegetable garden, saving these snails he made escargot every other Sunday evening so that he didn't have to share.

There was a possibility that these ties with Grandchildren were only enforced by the parents. I really hoped that this was the case. I was growing tired of listening to the man.

'I suppose it's mainly just from the women I been hearin' this,' Greg's bulldog lips said. 'They hit me and then bake me cakes, accuse me a' thieving the vegetables, then thank me for my apple crumble... They even say they hear me braggin' about how I steal Jewish people's bicycles! A white superman, Joan called me.'

Already having worked everything out in my head, my contemplative-style face went by rushed and fake.

'And lemme tell you the weird part,' Greg said. 'The other day up comes this fellah from the floor below, man from two-eleven asking me if I'm a psycho-something-or-other... Tellin' me he's been havin' lots'a trouble from people thinkin' he was a Neo-Nazi in the Tour de France.'

'MPD is the name for what you have,' I said.

I gave time for the acronym to baffle him.

Greg's lips gestured again and again over the three letters, his eyes meandering up to the left.

'Mary's Pupil Disease? Manic Paptest Disorder? Mucus Paternity Diagnosis? Gosh I hope it's not that one!' he thought.

'Multiple personality disorder,' I told him. 'And, prepare yourself... You're not the only one to come to me about this... It could very well be an epidemic.'

'Really?' Greg asked.

'Yes, really!' I said. 'Go to the head nurse, make-sure, make-sure, make-sure she hears all about this... Avoid public areas... What's your room number?'

'Th-three eleven?'

'Okay Greg,' I said, now covering my mouth and nose with my sweater. 'I don't want to catch this off you. I'm probably the only one who can get a cure, so you have to leave... And stay alert, Greg!'

I showed Greg the door and he hobbled out, affirmative but baffled.

'Could this kill me?' he asked.

'This could very well mean The Death of Pineview Inn,' I said.

My name in the Gossip Lounge on fourth floor was 'the man by the extinguisher', which is where every number-eleven apartment was situated on every floor of the ten-story building. Greg's room, three-eleven, was across from a large and candy-orange fire extinguisher. The man that had come to see Greg at Greg's room, two-eleven, was across from a large and candy-orange fire extinguisher, as well.

United by gossip, ten parallel universes operated like ten adaptations of the same play but with a different cast and crew on each floor. Throughout the building there had been talk of white-supremacist cyclists and gratitude shown to others who did not bake apple crumble for anybody.

The next day I was in a downtown park meeting a woman wearing a puffy white parka. Trying hard to find just one joint to smoke I met this bronze-tanned girl who happened to grow it. She was telling me how she once saw this orange pigeon squabbling about for food, right here. How peculiar.

'It's a new evolutionary adaptation,' I said, my brows set high on my head. 'Allows birds to camouflage with neon advertising.'

'Huh,' she said.

Ended up at her house for the night. All I told Lara was that my place was just a bit bedraggled. Meanwhile her one-room apartment was a damp garden with two fat jungle cats, overhead lights on high-beams all night, woke up with a tan, black stockings tied around my head to keep out the brightness, the pale shadow of Lara's arm, fried across my stomach... Left in the afternoon with a big bag full of plant seeds, high as a kite, seemed darker outside, lipstick on both cheeks.

That's not how it happens, just how it happened, then...

And at Pineview Inn I took the elevator up one floor at a time.

At every orange fire extinguisher I pivoted left, told the person that lived there the secret to curing MPD.

Plant these, lots of these here seeds plant them in your homes and in the garden outside. I will be around to pick them myself when they are budding, cure them and then cure you... We can only hope...

When I was just a seventeen year-old child I knew not to trust my love. I'm convinced it was parenting that taught me how to be so sceptical.

Anyone I'd met, any friends I'd had, any pets I'd loved I'd ask myself:

'You'd still kill'em for a million, right?'

When the answer was a swift, guttural, "NO!" I'd move on to the next question, and on with the scepticism.

'If you could've never met them for a million, would'ya?'

And it's sad to say, but no one's ever been the cause for a 'yes' answer.

My Mom was Town Slut... Father, as far as I know, was a Hit Man. They worked pretty well together, and I learned some things from the both of them...

Later on that night a woman began sobbing within the building. Sobbing and screaming because she was old and no one ever called her on the phone.

Laying awake, I imagined Lara stood there in the total static darkness of my bedroom.

'Either kill me or make me most alive,' I whispered to her apparition.

All that I have ever asked for. In her hand was an object, a phallic knife.

And so one day a Haitian gang came to The Pineview Inn. A

Haitian gang from Haiti, that is. They approached the garden of marijuana, which was now growing tall.

With slow, deliberate steps across the backyard as if to ensure that every blade of grass in their footsteps was dead...

Greg stood his ground in a white t-shirt, ended up in a fist-fight over the plants he was tending to, protecting them.

I could hear them asking the man who was in charge. I could hear Greg trying to remember my name, stuttering.

He was protecting *the cure*... And I didn't step in. And old man Greg ended up in hospital that night.

I went to see him with apple crumble, but did I really care? I sat in the waiting room.

Time went by.

Did I really care...?

Well... Greg did rank high in the wealth plot of Pineview.

No. No one's ever been the cause of a 'yes' answer. After all, in the hospital gown, this old man was looking better than ever.

Black-eye, no-teeth, no-hair, liver-warts, broken-wrist... Hands covered in dirt and youth. He jabbed the air from the gurney, told the tale to everyone through those great lips of his. He asked me to look after the plants, *the cure*. He gabbed fast and urgent and I nodded.

Saw one of Mrs. Drydell's birds, a red pigeon in the gutter, on my way to Lara's house. My bag overstuffed with harvested buds and all of my life possessions, another apple crumble in my lap kept my legs warm through a cold evening bus ride. The cold stirred itself into a storm, turned into rain and washed all that red off like blood off my hands.

I came to her door with my apple crumble and an eighty-one year-old daffodil in full-white bloom.

When I was nineteen I moved to New Orleans and lived at Pineview Retirement Inn. It was home because home was cheap and smelt like death and Grandparents.

FRESHERS
by ROSALIND WYLLIE

I 'M at this party, a student thing, and everyone is drinking and behaving in that pantomime way that they do; the whole flirting, pretending to be more drunk or less stoned than they actually are.

I don't even know whose house it is, and I don't know why I came – especially now they're playing a Sugababes CD. Everyone is dancing like this is proper music. So, I'm leaning against the wall, hating everyone in this room. I'm watching them all, the skinny jeaned girls dutifully wearing fake Ugg boots. Not an original thought under the two toned hair on their heads. The lads are just as bad, in combat trousers (so last year!) and raggedy band t-shirts, White Stripes, Babyshambles, Kings of Leon – stuff it's cool to like, though they probably listen to Queen when they're pissed.

These are the people I left home to avoid – it's like different faces, same bollocks, that sort of thing.

Everyone's copped off with someone, even though it's only day eleven. The first week the student bar was full of kids showing off and laughing too loud. This week it's all cliques and nicknames, couples holding hands like they've been together for years. Why so keen to be partnered up? Thousands of new people to choose from and they go getting heavy with the first person they meet.

Then Guy comes over and he says, 'Hey.' I don't look up, because I know who he is. Guy with his Diesel Jeans, black t-shirt and longish hair, but not ponytail long, if you get me. And he wears jewellery, a couple of chunky silver rings and a leather wristband, not that I've paid much attention.

The other girls have this whole drama about him. You know how those types can be, the ones whose voices pitch up a little the moment a good-looking boy comes into the room. They get giggly and develop a case of hair flicking Tourette's or something. Anyway, that's what they do around Guy.

'You live here?' He says and I shake my head, still not looking at him. I look instead at the frayed hem of my denim mini skirt, pleased that my St Tropez tan hasn't streaked, and pretend not to have heard him.

He nudges me gently, 'So that's not your prayer flag?' He nods towards a pink and purple wall hanging.

'Hardly,' I say, looking up briefly. He has long fingers, like a guitarist, his silver rings glinting.

'Coz for a moment there I figured we must be in Tibet, you know in some Buddhist community or something... I mean these are obviously very spiritual people eh?' I can hear that he's smiling and I sort of laugh.

He's got a point, the prayer flag overlooks fifty Freshers trying to cop of with each other, pissed up, coked up, stoned or whatever. The prayer flag, this year's student accessory, as obligatory as the Che Guevara poster on the stairs, the one next to Kurt Cobain.

'Beer?' he says and I say, 'Yes.' So he gets us a couple of bottles. He hands me mine, and swigs back on his. He doesn't try and clink bottles or anything, doesn't ask if he got the right sort, just leans back against the wall, not saying anything more. I think that maybe he's okay.

'They've got Kahil Gibran, in the toilet,' I say as he takes another swig, checking to see if he gets the reference. 'It's like they had a tick box of *integral items for student life*.'

Guy snorts beer back out through his nose. '*The Prophet*, man that's deep, these are deep people... they're really taxing themselves here, going for the hard stuff.' He laughs, wiping his face with his sleeve.

'He's the easy-listening artist of philosophy,' I reply.

'For the faux-spiritual,' he adds.

'A little hippy-lite.' I swig back on the bottle and we share a smile.

We move through to the kitchen, pick up a few more beers and then walk from room to room looking for somewhere to sit down, somewhere to talk. We wind up in the bathroom, sat side by side, on the edge of the bath.

'We're in the same cognitive theory class right?' he asks so I shrug and say, 'I think so, yes.'

'You from down here?' I ask and he sort of looks at me and then says, 'Yeah, mainly... well, not London but a suburban hellhole about forty miles out... a housing estate with a crappy shopping precinct, you know the kind of place... dull, dull, dull...you?'

'Newcastle,' I reply and he nods, 'I figured.' I wait for him to make some dumb joke about Geordies and Mackems or try to mimic my accent. But he doesn't.

The bathroom is too bright and I'm trying not to look in the mirrors, don't want to look like I'm the sort of girl who thinks too much about her appearance. But my reflection is looking at me over Guy's shoulder. I try hard to look natural but it's really disconcerting. My makeup looks okay, but my hair needs brushing. I twist a few strands in my fingers and look again at my beer bottle.

'Want to go somewhere else?' he says.

We go back to mine. Guy says he's in a flat share with like a million other boys and that his room is, 'fucking disgusting, the sooner I find my own place the better.'

We walk, because it's only ten minutes away, and the weather is cool but not wet. He doesn't hold my hand or anything, but we keep sort of bumping into each other as we're walking along.

In the shop he buys a four pack of Stella and a bottle of wine, I go to give him some money but he says, 'I'll get it, not a problem.' But then he has to ask me to give him a couple of quid coz the wine isn't as cheap as he had hoped. Even though he's embarrassed about it he sort of laughs and I tease him a little, giving him a friendly shove and he kind of shoves me back and grins.

I'm living in 'halls'. My room is tiny, just a single bed, desk and drawers. There's a rack of books, and a laptop that my Dad gave me – my leaving home gift.

Guy checks out my CDs and chooses a John Martyn CD, while I borrow a corkscrew from Sarah next door. Sarah winks and makes a face, like she knows what I'm up to. Normally it would piss me off, but I let it pass, because I'm having a good night.

Guy looks at the photos on my pin board while I push my cuddly toys under the bed.

'These your parents?' He points to a picture of my Mum and Dad.

'What are they like?'

'Oh God, don't get me started.' I imagine taking Guy home to meet them. I can't wait to take him down to The Free Trade, and show him off to my old school friends, they will be so jealous.

'What do they do?'

'My Dad… well… he's like totally embarrassing. He works for an insurance company… accounts manager or something tedious, and my Mum… used to be a teacher but now she teaches piano… private tutorials that sort of thing.'

'Oh do you play? God I would love to play… I play the guitar… a little… well... I'm pretty crap actually… but I like to pretend I'm Hendrix… you know…' Guy sits on the end of the bed, not too close, not too far. He takes a small pouch out of his pocket. 'Do you want a smoke?' I nod, though I don't usually do dope, but hey, this is university. The start of my whole new life.

'The piano lessons kind of didn't work out,' I say and make a face. 'I refused to practice… my mother's still mad at me… thinks I did it to spite her.'

'Your petty act of rebellion?' Guy smiles.

'Something like that… maybe, I didn't want to end up like her.'

Guy looks again at the photo. 'She looks nice… pretty… you look a little like her… younger obviously.' He winks at me when he says this and I bite my lip.

'My Mum listens to Maria Carey and Celine Dion. She cries at Julia Roberts movies… she's fine… she's in bed by ten o'clock every night.' Guy is stroking my hand. I should stop talking, but instead I carry on and on. 'She's like two stone overweight and me and my brother are her whole life. She's never done anything you know… never travelled, just package holidays twice a year… whatever's on offer at Thomas Cook… I… want… well… something… you know, Goa, Nepal, adventures… something more… know what I mean?'

Guy leans forward and I think for a moment that he is going to kiss me, but he pulls a book from the shelf instead and uses it to balance his Rizla.

'I know exactly what you mean.' With a quick flick of his wrist he has the joint ready to light.

We lean from the window smoking the joint and looking out over the campus. Our shoulders squash together. The campus lights glow orange and yellow over the pathways and we watch the couples and groups below. The packs of lads are yelling and singing *Bohemian Rhapsody*. Pissed up girls stagger below barefoot, stilettos hanging from their hands.

'This song is my total favourite,' he says when *May You Never* comes on.

'Wow. No... mine too... seriously.'

Guy leans his hand on mine.

'I read *The Prophet* once,' I say. 'My Mum gave it to me, they used some of it their wedding or something... for a while there I thought it was like totally deep, like eye opening.'

'Me too.' He laughs. 'I used to quote it. I drove my parents mad quoting stuff at them.' You may give your children your love but not your thoughts.' I thought I was so clever.' Guy and I smile. We are a conspiracy.

'You may strive to be like them, but seek not to make them like you,' I say with mock gravitas.

Guy pushes his hair away from his eyes. 'Oh God, imagine... I even had a prayer wheel, I'm serious... when I was fifteen I was like a serious Buddhist... sat in my room chanting *Om Mani Padme* Hum and lighting incense.'

'But you grew out of it?'

'Yeah, I got interested in girls and suddenly a life of abstinence and mantras seemed less appealing.'

'Do you think it's all phases?' I say. 'Like, are we ever going to have a new experience or has it all been done before, I mean is this is it? Are we just repeating stuff?'

'Shit, one joint and suddenly you're talking like a real student.'

'Sorry,' I say, and he shrugs and gives me back the joint, 'No, I like it, have a little more... see whether we get onto reincarnation or existentialism.'

'I just want... you know...'

Which is when he kisses me and even though he tastes of smoke and Stella, and even though I think closing your eyes when you kiss is total bollocks, I close my eyes.

When I open them again he is looking at me, smiling.

'Sorry 'bout that,' he says. 'Couldn't help myself... Rude to interrupt... You were saying?'

'It doesn't matter...'

'No... Tell me, what were you saying?' His arm moves over my shoulder proprietarily, like I'm his now. I loop my thumb into the back pocket of his jeans.

'I want to be different... you know... that's all... do something... be something new,' I say, feeling the words catch in my throat.

'Me too,' he says, his face a wide-open smile. 'Me too.'

COME WALK WITH ME ON THE WILD SIDE, SWEET JESUS
by P.A. TANTON

ROB, you are one cr-razy mother,' Steve laughed between puffs of smoke.

Rob had just finished explaining to Steve and Beto for the last time that if the Confederate States of America had won the Civil War, then things in Knoxville wouldn't be so screwed up. With his jaw wired shut, Rob's elocution became increasingly waterlogged as his delivery grew more impassioned. The only things that he could pronounce without sending a spray of saliva through the room were racial slurs, which comprised most of his vocabulary.

'Now I don't mind these foreign exchange students coming over, because they'll all probably mostly leave, and some o' them European girls are pretty damn hot.' He rubbed his near-bald head in frustration, his hand passing over the peach fuzz, feeling the result of a communication error with the barber earlier in the day.

Steve passed the pipe to Beto, who re-filled it and took a long hit before handing it on to Rob.

At first Rob didn't see it, as Beto was sitting on his blind side, his eye puffed up as the result of another communication error with a guy in the bar the previous night.

'Beto, you sonofabitch, you've already smoked this bowl down,' he spat.

'Dude, there's plenty left. Let me have another hit.'

'Fuck off.'

Rob jammed the pipe into the side of his mouth and sucked.

'Man, you look like Popeye,' Steve laughed again, and this time Beto laughed too.

Rob grabbed his crotch in response, his good eye glowing with indignation.

'You guys ready for the party?' Steve asked.

'Can't. Got church tomorrow,' Rob grunted, trying not to let the smoke escape from his mouth.

'Rob, you are one cr-razy mother,' Beto repeated, smacking his lips and looking for his jacket.

'Never heard of an evangelical Catholic, you sure you aren't really a Baptist?' Steve said.

'Eat me.'

'Cr-razy,' said Beto.

Rob followed them outside. He would have liked to have gone to the party. There would be girls there, but the two hits of acid he had taken on top of the ecstasy and beer were beginning to kick in. He already felt guilty about it and was struggling to remember when he had last gone to confession. The painkillers he was on for his jaw must be playing with his memory. There was no telling what sins he still had outstanding, although most of them were probably only venal. No mortal sins yet that he could think of, although the excesses of the past couple of days were beginning to catch up with him.

Steve couldn't find his keys, Beto needed the bathroom. Rob lay back on the hood of the car while the other two went back inside, muttering to himself a passage from Joshua that he used whenever someone got him on the topic of the Civil War:

'Now therefore you are cursed, and some of you shall always be slaves, hewers of wood and drawers of water for the house of my God.'

Everyone was cursed. Hell in a handbasket. He stuck his lighter into the bowl of the pipe and inhaled.

The sky was moody, the nights were beginning to feel warm again, but the spring storms kept blowing in clouds and even against the interference of the street lights the full moon cast an eerie red glow. A red moon, a killing moon. A big eye in the sky. A big eye staring down. A big blinking eye staring down at him. An eye. Blinking repeatedly. Watching him.

'Dude, got the keys. Let's move.' Steve slapped Rob's shin, causing him to jump up and send the pipe flying into the shadows.

'Goddamn. What'd you do that for?' Rob growled.

'Man, that's some crazy shit there, Rob. You sure you're okay?'

'Yeah, just give me a lift down to Cherokee Avenue.'

He was not okay. The moon had just blinked at him. The all-seeing eye had just probed the inner depths of his soul. He was sure neither Steve nor Beto would have seen it, or understood. They were the unrepentant.

On Twenty-first street, despite his mortal fear, he found himself looking at the moon again through the rear window of Steve's car. It was not just an eyeball, it was an eyeball made up of several eyes, all looking at him.

'Holy shit. Steve, if you want to save your soul, Beto man, you too, then stop the car and pray with me. Right now.'

'Rob, I'm in traffic, man. You are majorly stoned, aren't you?' Steve chuckled. His good humor was beginning to really annoy Rob. Beto turned around in the passenger seat to get a good look at him.

'Don't look at me, man. Look at the fucking moon. *"...I saw a Lamb standing, as though it had been slain, with seven horns and with seven eyes, which are the seven spirits of God sent out into all the earth..."* Jesus Christ, boys, this is it.' The Rapture, the Apocalypse, he was sure of it.

'He's going nuts?' Beto asked.

'Rob, you gonna be sick? Let me know and I'll pull over, man.'

They didn't understand. There was no way they would, there was no time. The moon-eye was looking at him, anyway. They'd had their chance to repent, just like he had. Of all the weeks to forget to go to confession. Damn painkillers.

His only option now was to escape. He could only save himself. The passing streetlights danced on the upholstry, turning the back seat into a paisley garden. The paisleys turned to dragons which roared silently and darkly. They had piercing eyes which grew and consumed the rest of their bodies, until all he saw was one eternal waterfall of unblinking eyes.

He threw himself from the car.

He landed on his shoulder in the glass-strewn edge of the road and went rolling off into a drainage ditch. Traffic stopped and people shouted, but he managed to clamber up out of the mud and into the woody undergrowth before anyone could get to him.

His shoulder and arm burned, but it was nothing compared to the burning that would come with the end of the world. Especially for someone who had missed confession.

He crashed through bushes, branches tearing at his flesh, the humid Tennessee night causing him to sweat even more profusely. The time was coming, and he was sorry for everything he had ever done, although he couldn't remember anything specific.

His pulse quickened, and his heart climbed into his throat. He stopped in front of a dancing tree, which paused long enough for him to urinate against it.

He needed to cleanse himself, to make himself pure. The nearest water was down at the river. The quickest route was through the expensive houses along Cherokee Avenue.

Traffic screeched to a halt as he bounded back out of the undergrowth and over the avenue towards the floodlit lawns of Cherokee Heights.

He discarded his shoes and flung them into a flower bed. The moist ground felt soft between his toes, which he stubbed against a lawn sprinkler. Jumping over a fence, he came to a swimming pool. It might do until he reached the river. He shed the rest of his clothes and jumped in with a mighty splash. His bloody shoulder stung when it reacted with the chlorine in the pool. When he surfaced there were lights and the sounds of barking.

Hounds of Hell, the Lion of the Tribe of Judah, something unearthly, he didn't know what, was coming for him.

He pulled himself from the pool and continued frantically in the direction of the river. Back into the open, he ran into the street, repeating the Hail Mary while gasping for breath. A car full of girls honked at him. Thinking this was the trumpet sounding the tearing of the temple curtain, he tore back off across the lawn of a big house, where he lost control and went skidding into the hood of a parked Volvo, winding himself. As he lay on the driveway, the car alarm went off.

Summoning the unbelievable strength of the Righteous, he stood up and carried on, blocking out the sounds of shouting, the Voices of the Damned.

He heard hooves, the thunder of horses.

'Jesus Christ almighty, forgive me!'

Completely naked, he neared the river, light dancing all around him. The wind blew, the thundering got louder and closer, voices sang down to him from Heaven.

Then there was peace.

'Wake up, punk.'

A golden haze of light leaked in under Rob's eyelids and as

he came to he found he was not, as he had expected, staring face-to-face with the Angel of Death, but peering eyeball-to-serial number at the badge of a Knoxville police officer. The Tennessee state flag was sewn over the officer's pocket, and the various insignia on his uniform caught the light and emitted an other-worldly glimmer that made Rob continue to wonder if he was really dead.

'Wake up, you piece of shit.'

A second officer was now patting his cheek. Realising that he was still very much alive, Rob lurched forward only to find that he was strapped to a bed, still naked.

'Where am I?' he tried to say, forgetting that his jaw was wired shut.

The officers didn't answer.

'He's delirious,' one of them said.

'He'll understand this – one count of public indecency, one count of vagrancy, two possible counts of disturbing the peace, and there was a homicide last night that we could pin on you.'

The two policemen stared down at him. Standard issue cops, stupid and fat, looking to meet their arrest quota.

'You gonna confess?'

Just two officers, four pairs of eyes; dull, unfeeling, unscary eyes. The moon was gone, replaced by what appeared to be hospital equipment. The world was safe for the moment, the end postponed. Rob heaved a sigh of relief.

'You gonna confess?' the officer repeated.

Rob shook his head.

The first officer leaned in menacingly.

'Then tell us who you are.'

Rob's face relaxed into the smile of the sinner given a second chance and said, 'One cr-razy mother.'

THE GOOD PROVIDER
by STEVE WHEELER

I **CLEAN** the cream from my whiskers with my paw. I sit watching the delicious little birds hop from seed to seed on the dying thistles, in the garden, outside the window. This window seat is made for these lazy autumn afternoons. Red'll be home soon. I love to watch his change of expression when he approaches the house to greet his latest wife. She's Lola this year. It was Linda back in those days, Bennie's sister. It's getting harder to remember that I used to live with Bennie.

The boys came up with the idea, in a poker game, at Bennie's. There was Mutt, Jeff, Bennie and Slocum. I watched from the back of the couch, cleaning my paws with my tongue. There were clouds of smoke, interesting smells, emanating from the table that night. The boys were flying high. Bennie figured his ship had finally come in.

The next morning, as we drove to work, Bennie talked about the score. He talked to me, but he was really talking to himself. He was a good provider though, so I went along with it.

Bennie was my owner, a cat worshipper, who also owned

Brutus, a watchdog. Bennie took me to work with him, most days. I was an excuse for Bennie to talk to himself, a warm body to have around.

Bennie was the only employee left in Red Smith's auto parts warehouse. Red didn't make much, wholesaling used auto parts, but he had a famous safe. The safe made Red a tidy profit. He held payrolls for a lot of companies which didn't have the facilities to handle large amounts of cash. They couldn't fit into bank schedules. The safe also held such items as receipts, estates, and some money from questionable sources which Red labeled, 'Other'.

On the way to work, the next morning, Bennie dreamed along with the sports show on the radio.

'With my cut, I could buy an island, like Brando. Down in Tahiti. So what if he's fat? Women still love him. I'd have a party for the boys, but not for a couple of years. This is Slocum's chance, too. He can escape from his old lady, finally. The guy's not well. She's a bad influence. Don't you think he's shrunk and turned grey since he's been with her?'

I sat in the back seat watching some dogs on the sidewalk. Gross. Brutus ran out when Bennie opened the front door of the warehouse. There are dogs and there are dirty dogs. Brutus was dirty and aggressive with everyone except Bennie and me. Bennie had trained him; I had shown him my claws, when we first met. He almost lost an eye that time, always respected me since. I wouldn't turn my back on him, though.

Brutus is big. He's a big, dirty watchdog who would tear anything apart, just for fun. Unless someone killed Brutus or otherwise incapacitated him, they'd never be able to steal from this warehouse. Unless they had an in and knew how the safe worked, that is.

Bennie was counting on this, as part of his plan. He could control Brutus and retirement was approaching. If he ripped the place off, he could sit tight for a few years, let things cool down.

If everyone kept their mouths shut and they paid a lawyer Mutt knew, they would all end up rich. Even Red had some kind of insurance for a robbery, Bennie figured, but it wasn't an urgent consideration. Red could afford it, no doubt.

There would be questions. There would be all kinds of cops. They would insist on a lie detector test, but he didn't have to take it, they couldn't use it in court.

Brando never backed down from a role. This was one for which Bennie had been preparing all of his life. That was the way Bennie saw it, anyway. I always thought he was a little crazy, but who could have known?

The safe only opened once a day. If robbers did get past Brutus and the other alarms, unless they came at exactly the right time, they would have to blow the door off of it. It would take a big explosion to blow the door, neighbouring alarms would go off all over the place. There wasn't much paper around, but there might be a fire. The other thing, which only Red knew about the safe, but no one else knew, was that it expelled all of the oxygen, slowly, out of itself, after the door closed. Red got it from an art museum when the government closed it down.

One of the perks of having a foolproof safe was that big companies were advised, by word of mouth, to use Red's, in emergencies. Red made a pretty penny helping out big companies.

When the boys thought up the plan at the poker game, it was after Bennie had told them all about the 'special job' Red was doing that weekend. A big company was moving millions of dollars from city to city. They were leaving it in Red's safe, overnight, on the weekend. Bennie and the boys planned to rip it off.

I stretched, tasted the fresh cat food Bennie had left in my dish, by the office door. I settled in the comfortable window, watched Bennie strike poses in front of the mirror. Every time I cleaned the outside of my ears, I remembered the ticks. Getting rid of them was a painful process.

Bennie thought he looked like Brando when he practised a sneer. I thought he looked like an overweight Elvis impersonator. There was an inventory to keep, some paperwork to do, but Bennie mostly listened to a redneck on the radio, talked to me, during his work day. When we were at the warehouse, Bennie kept Brutus in his run, outside, in the back.

Red dropped in on Friday afternoon, for a few minutes. He ruffled my fur, scratched my ears. Red was just getting to like me, in those days. He went over the delivery of the money on Saturday morning, told Bennie that he had Sunday off, that he, Red, would be there to make sure of the pick up on Sunday morning.

Red sat in Bennie's chair, feet up, smoking a cigar, called Linda. He put Bennie on with his sister, enjoyed their fraternal banter. Red glowed with love for Linda. His face changed when he talked to her on the phone. When he spoke about her with Bennie, the latter thought he was kidding. Bennie looked at Red, quizzically, behind his back, after these conversations about his older sister.

The boys planned to pull into the warehouse as soon as the delivery was made on Saturday morning. They would load the money, take it away. They would leave Bennie in the safe, to be released by Red, the next day. The story would be that the robbers showed up right after the security company delivered the cash, pushed Bennie into the safe, left with the loot and the security film. The key to getting away with it, was for everyone to behave normally. These guys thought they could pull it off.

It sounded good, that night, when the boys met for poker at our place. Mutt had all the papers and powers of attorney for them to sign. It would give their lawyer, who wasn't above a bit of graft himself, the right to move their money around. No one could quit their jobs or do anything out of the ordinary for, at least, two years. They were all thinking about retirement. The boys were closer to old than young.

The delivery Saturday morning went smoothly; the security company guards moved the cash into the safe. They had just pulled out of the parking lot when Mutt, Jeff and Slocum pulled up, at the front door, in Slocum's black van.

Bennie had already taken the film out of all the security cameras when they walked into the office. They wore gloves, but no masks or disguises. Bennie showed them the millions of dollars they were stealing by opening a package. They got lost in a delirious minute of congratulations while they admired the bills.

After a short debate, they figured that I should keep Bennie company in the safe. There was nothing soft and warm inside the safe. I never did like it. They threw me in, with Bennie, after they put my dish and some water inside the door. I circled the safe quickly, ran out, just as they slammed the door shut.

They left him some chocolate bars and water, but they couldn't do anything about the light. There was no light, but Bennie planned to sleep, rehearse his shock and anger until Red arrived, anyway. They didn't even notice me until it was too late. No one had time to worry about me, so they left.

The three of them giggled as they got into Slocum's van. In a few years, they would be on easy street. Margaritas all around at Bennie's place, in Tahiti, one island over from Brando's. All they had to do now was to drop off the money at the lawyer's.

At the time, I didn't know, nobody did, except Red, about the slow leak of oxygen from the safe. Bennie must have realized that something was wrong because he made a lot of noise in the safe around the same time that Red arrived, the next morning.

Red's Cadillac pulled up beside Bennie's Celebrity in the empty parking lot. I watched from the front window as Red got out of his car, walked toward the building. He looked back once at Bennie's car. He was about half way between his parking space and the warehouse, when his cell phone went off.

He dug it out of his jacket pocket, answered it. I could tell that he was talking to a woman he loved by the change of expression on Red's face. It lit up.

He stopped, looked at the sky as he talked. He had a big smile on his face when he turned back to the car. He listened to the phone, smiled at his shoes.

Red got back into his Caddy, talking on the phone, his eyes on Bennie's Celebrity. He was talking to Lola that day. He thought Bennie had his days off mixed up, so that he was taking care of the pick up. He was partially right, Bennie was there, but he was in the safe.

The noises from the safe got fewer and further between, quieter, then stopped all together. Brutus started howling and whining from the back of the warehouse. Brando's death scene in *The Godfather* always was one of Bennie's favourites, but I think he would rather have played it in a tomato patch.

When the security guys from the pick up company arrived, there was no one around. They called Red. They told him that they could see the cat in the office window and that Bennie's car was there, but no Bennie.

By this time I was hungry, the litter box was filling up. I knew, from Brutus's mournful howl, that Bennie had, somehow, died in the safe.

Red drove over from Lola's the next morning. He took a long time calling long distance, pushing digital codes to open the safe before its special time.

Red's reputation was on the line. The reputation of his service to the big companies. The security company had to have the money.

Red breathed through his nose a lot, walked around the office with a serious expression, followed by the security guards, talking into their cell phones. If they had arrived earlier, if Red hadn't taken so long to open the safe, they could have seen Bennie gasping for his last breath.

The police were called as soon as Red opened the door, found Bennie dead in the safe, the money gone.

Red seemed surprised and a little hurt by the discovery of

Bennie's body. When he saw the cat dishes of water and food, inside the safe door, he adopted me, on the spot. He took me home to his very comfortable estate. It was as if he was protecting me. He switched from Linda to Lola, just after Bennie's funeral. Linda accused him of holding out on her, but Red paid her off. It wasn't the payment she wanted, but she had to settle for it.

The police questioned all of Bennie's friends. Nobody talked. No one was caught for the theft.

Lola's a real cat lover so I'm pampered and lazy here. There are no poker games with smoke and interesting smells, but the food is great. Yesterday she got some cat treats and served them to me on a pillow. It gets harder and harder to remember life at Bennie's.

Red suffered his loss manfully, in public. Bennie's death was so shocking that Red's compensation from the insurance company went unnoticed.

Red doesn't know Mutt or Jeff or Slocum. They don't move in the same circles. They were all there at Bennie's funeral, also attended by a large number of undercover cops. I watched from the passenger seat of Red's Caddy.

When it was over, they filed past the Cadillac, on their way to the cars.

Red argued with Linda over Bennie's grave.

Slocum looked me right in the eye, winked as he passed the windshield. He knew that I had seen it all and that Red was a good provider.

ABOUT THE CONTRIBUTORS

KIRSTEN BERGEN was born in Vancouver, but has spent most of her life abroad. She is a trained translator and interpreter, and worked in the Paris region and in southern Germany in various office-based jobs before teaching Business English and translating. She started writing about two years ago and lives in northern Germany with her husband and baby daughter.

DAVID BRECKENRIDGE has been writing for years, and has always been a daydreamer, through work and through schools. Besides writing poems and short stories, he is also writing scripts, yearning to be an amateur filmmaker, animating, photographing, and he also plays a lot of improvisational piano, sometimes with other jammers.

PAUL BROWN is a freelance writer who has published scores of magazine features and three non-fiction books, the latest being *The Rocketbelt Caper* in 2005. He holds an MA in Creative Writing from the University of Northumbria, and lives by the banks of the River Tyne. He is a publishing editor at Tonto Press.

FIONA CASE grew up in Devon and Cornwall, and moved to London in 1989. After a varied career, she is in the process of retraining to be barrister – and will probably specialise in criminal law. She has been writing fiction as a hobby since her teens, although only started sending it out into the world a few years ago.

ELIZA HEMINGWAY was born in the West Riding of Yorkshire, but now writes short stories and novels on Vancouver Island, Canada. She has written for newspapers, acted on stage and in films and read stories for CBC Radio. She was made an Honorary Citizen of Victoria for her work in the arts.

JOLENE HUI is a writer/actor who loves to watch TV, eat sweets, and dream of the day when she will get her Chinese Crested Hairless and Standard Poodle so that she can finally have the family she always desired. She currently resides in San Diego with her writer/actor/musician boyfriend.

SAM JACKSON was encouraged to write by a work colleague who, while applauding her unwavering commitment to the notion of a paperless office, felt that conveying telephone messages through mime was perhaps not the solution the world of commerce had been waiting for. Sam is a part-time clerical officer, devoting the remainder of her time to creative writing and retail therapy.

PHIL JELL was born in 1978. He trained at art school and later at the Courtauld Institute, where he decided writing fiction was more interesting than researching for a Masters degree. He has been a photographer, TV scene-painter, gardener and just about everything else to keep himself in ink and paper. Phil currently works and lives in South London.

BERNARD LANDRETH is a retired civil engineer. He has had poetry published in many anthologies and broadcast on BBC radio. He has also won a number of prizes in poetry competitions. *The Slug* is his first published short story.

For the last two years, **ROBIN MARSDEN** has been living and writing in Barcelona. Recently, he has moved to London, where he is working on a novel.

ADAM MAXWELL lives in the North East of England where he spends his timing drinking coffee (not tea). He would gladly sell his soul to Starbucks if they asked him but until this happens he is working on his writing. If you like liked his story you can read more of them by going to his website www.jigsawlounge.co.uk.

After graduating from Magdalen College, Oxford, where he studied with the poet John Fuller, **NICK MONTGOMERY** joined the band Microdisney, a John Peel favourite, recording and touring in the UK and Europe. He was awarded a Doctorate in 2000 from Newcastle University for a thesis on Virginia Woolf. He is currently working on a novel, *Milk of Amnesia*, and a screenplay with the artist Tracey Tofield.

SAM MORRIS lives in the rural wilds of Kent, which he likes to explore. When he's not lost or too covered in mud to be admitted into the house, he likes to write. He has been previously published in several e-zines, but this is his first excursion into print.

STEPHEN SHIEBER's lust for glory was awakened at an early age, when, in 1980, he won first prize in a Methodist colouring-in contest. He suffers from an irrational fear of barbershops. Born in Germany, Stephen has little desire to travel, but recommends holidaying in Finland. He lives in Newcastle-upon-Tyne, where he works as a cod philosopher at a local school.

P.A. TANTON's writing is influenced by his childhood growing up in the Southern US as well as his experiences as a travelling violin salesman, stockroom worker for a London publisher, and itinerant bicycle racer. His novel, *Johnny Lonely*, was selected as a Fresh Fiction Prediction at the New Writing North Fresh Fiction Festival in 2004. As an American teaching English in a Gateshead school, he is a walking, talking lesson in irony.

DAVID WATSON has been writing fiction on and off – mainly off – for around twenty years. He works as a creative director and will continue to do so until he's snapped up by a publishing house with pockets deep enough to fund his lavish lifestyle. He's aiming to complete his first novel, *Savage Amusement*, in 2006.

LUKE WATSON graduated from Leeds University with a degree in Creative Writing. He lives in Gloucestershire.

STUART WHEATMAN has a MA in Creative Writing from Northumbria University. He lives in the North East of England and has an interest in popular culture and modernism, and is a publishing editor at Tonto Press.

STEVE WHEELER is a graduate of Carleton University in Ottawa and a lifelong fan of good rock 'n roll, blues and some jazz. He has lived in Western Canada, Asia, Europe and the USA. He is presently living with his wife Ellie in the suburbs of Ottawa, and enjoying the hockey season.

ROSALIND WYLLIE was born in 1970 and has a degree in Psychology from London Guildhall University and a Masters in Creative Writing from Northumbria University. She has worked as a drugs counsellor, community development worker and a factory packer. She now works part time for social services. She recently completed a novel and her first stage play *Green Beans* is being staged in 2006.

ABOUT TONTO PRESS

TONTO Press is an independent publishing concern based in the North East of England. Formed in 2005 by authors Paul Brown and Stuart Wheatman, Tonto offers new writers more opportunities and a fairer deal than traditional publishers.

The *Tonto Short Stories* project launched Tonto's search for new writing talent.

Tonto Short Stories is supported by Arts Council England.

Tonto Press is named after the sidekick of the Lone Ranger, the popular Western character. Tonto was the son of a chief in the Potawatomi nation, and his name translates as 'Wild One' in his own language. He was famously portrayed on television by Jay Silverheels. Tonto's horse was a spotted palomino named Scout.

For further information about Tonto Press and our projects please see www.tontopress.com.

Printed in the United Kingdom
by Lightning Source UK Ltd.
108422UKS00001B/7-66